S0-BXZ-345

ONCE WAS NOT ENOUGH

The first time Melody Clemm came into Skye Fargo's arms, he had no idea of the tortures her family meted out to the legion of men who had dared to make love to this voluptuous vixen.

He knew now—and counted himself lucky to have gotten out of their clutches with a whole skin.

Yet here she was again, telling him, "Skye, whatever the rest of the family's been doing is no concern of mine."

Could she be serious?

She was serious about one thing, at least. She pulled her scanty nightgown over her head and stood with her incredibly inviting body open to his gaze, her lips half-parted in lust. *Hell*, Skye thought, reaching out for her, *one more time can't hurt*.

How wrong could the Trailsman be about something that felt so right?

Ø SIGNET WESTERNS BY JOHN SHARPE

FOLLOW THE TRAILSMAN

(0451)

☐ THE TRAILSMAN #1: SEVEN WAGONS WEST   (127293—$2.50)*
☐ THE TRAILSMAN #2: THE HANGING TRAIL   (132939—$2.50)*
☐ THE TRAILSMAN #3: MOUNTAIN MAN KILL   (121007—$2.50)
☐ THE TRAILSMAN #4: THE SUNDOWN SEARCHERS   (122003—$2.50)
☐ THE TRAILSMAN #5: THE RIVER RAIDERS   (111990—$2.25)
☐ THE TRAILSMAN #6: DAKOTA WILD   (119886—$2.50)
☐ THE TRAILSMAN #7: WOLF COUNTRY   (123697—$2.50)
☐ THE TRAILSMAN #8: SIX-GUN DRIVE   (121724—$2.50)
☐ THE TRAILSMAN #9: DEAD MAN'S SADDLE   (126629—$2.50)*
☐ THE TRAILSMAN #10: SLAVE HUNTER   (124987—$2.50)
☐ THE TRAILSMAN #11: MONTANA MAIDEN   (116321—$2.50)*
☐ THE TRAILSMAN #12: CONDOR PASS   (118375—$2.50)*
☐ THE TRAILSMAN #13: BLOOD CHASE   (119274—$2.50)*
☐ THE TRAILSMAN #14: ARROWHEAD TERRITORY   (120809—$2.50)*
☐ THE TRAILSMAN #15: THE STALKING HORSE   (121430—$2.50)*
☐ THE TRAILSMAN #16: SAVAGE SHOWDOWN   (122496—$2.50)*
☐ THE TRAILSMAN #17: RIDE THE WILD SHADOW   (122801—$2.50)*

*Prices slightly higher in Canada

Buy them at your local bookstore or use this convenient coupon for ordering.

NEW AMERICAN LIBRARY,
P.O. Box 999, Bergenfield, New Jersey 07621

Please send me the books I have checked above. I am enclosing $_____
(please add $1.00 to this order to cover postage and handling). Send check
or money order—no cash or C.O.D.'s. Prices and numbers are subject to change
without notice.

Name_____

Address_____

City_____ State_____ Zip Code_____
Allow 4-6 weeks for delivery.
This offer is subject to withdrawal without notice.

THE TRAILSMAN 54

KILLER CLAN

by

Jon Sharpe

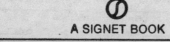

A SIGNET BOOK

NEW AMERICAN LIBRARY

NAL BOOKS ARE AVAILABLE AT QUANTITY DISCOUNTS
WHEN USED TO PROMOTE PRODUCTS OR SERVICES.
FOR INFORMATION PLEASE WRITE TO PREMIUM MARKETING DIVISION,
NEW AMERICAN LIBRARY, 1633 BROADWAY,
NEW YORK, NEW YORK 10019.

PUBLISHER'S NOTE

This novel is a work of fiction. Names, characters, places, and incidents either are the product of the author's imagination or are used fictitiously, and any resemblance to actual persons, living or dead, events, or locales is entirely coincidental.

Copyright © 1986 by Jon Sharpe

All rights reserved

The first chapter of this book previously appeared in *Longhorn Guns*, the fifty-third volume in this series.

SIGNET TRADEMARK REG. U.S. PAT. OFF. AND FOREIGN COUNTRIES
REGISTERED TRADEMARK—MARCA REGISTRADA
HECHO EN CHICAGO, U.S.A.

SIGNET, SIGNET CLASSIC, MENTOR, PLUME, MERIDIAN AND NAL BOOKS
are published by New American Library,
1633 Broadway, New York, New York 10019

First Printing, June, 1986

1 2 3 4 5 6 7 8 9

PRINTED IN THE UNITED STATES OF AMERICA

The Trailsman

Beginnings ... they bend the tree and they mark the man. Skye Fargo was born when he was eighteen. Terror was his midwife, vengeance his first cry. Killing spawned Skye Fargo, ruthless, cold-blooded murder. Out of the acrid smoke of gunpowder still hanging in the air, he rose, cried out a promise never forgotten.

The Trailsman, they began to call him, all across the West: searcher, scout, hunter, the man who could see where others only looked, his skills for hire but not his soul, the man who lived each day to the fullest, yet trailed each tomorrow. Skye Fargo, the Trailsman, the seeker who could take the wildness of a land and the wanting of a woman and make them his own.

*1861—Fort Larned and points west,
where a dark-haired siren lures unsuspecting
travelers into the blood-soaked bosom
of a mad family*

1

Fargo pulled his Pinto to a halt and gazed across the undulating swath of grassland at the hotel and the cluster of sheds and supply stores around it. Built of peeled logs and raw lumber, the unpainted structures stood out gauntly in the bright, late-afternoon sun.

At first glance it seemed pretty damn foolish to build a hotel in the middle of that empty sea of grass. But just beyond the hotel Fargo could see the sun-whitened trace of the Santa Fe Trail. According to Fort Larned's commanding officer, this hotel was perfectly situated to serve as a supply depot and a much-needed resting place for the steady stream of settlers using the trail on their way west.

Fargo nudged his Ovaro off the saddleback and kept to an easy lope as he traversed the long grassy swale fronting the compound. He was doing his best to contain his sense of urgency. If Lieutenant Becker was not off his feed, the two men Fargo had been seeking for the past six months were staying at this hotel, waiting to join a wagon train soon to be passing by on its way to Santa Fe.

Fargo pulled his pinto to a halt before the hotel and saw a long-necked gent step out of a barn to peer at him from under the brim of his straw hat. He was carrying a pitchfork and was dressed in filthy bib overalls. At the same time a round, cheery-looking woman, hastily wiping fresh flour off her hands, came out of the hotel door. Halting on the hotel porch, she beamed at Fargo.

"Welcome! Welcome! My land! It's so good to see a friendly face!"

Dismounting, Fargo dropped his reins over the hitch rack. "Thank you, ma'am," he replied.

Despite its rough-hewn exterior, the hotel impressed Fargo. The walls were solid, the windows spacious, and the veranda fronted the entire length of the building, its roof serving as a railed balcony.

A chunky, powerful-looking fellow stepped out onto the porch. He was the woman's son, no doubt about it. His resemblance to her was uncanny. The young man smiled broadly at Fargo, like someone trying to imitate the village idiot.

"Howdy, mister," he said heartily. "You sure are a welcome sight after that crazy Indian."

"Indian? What Indian?"

"He was just here an hour ago," the young

man replied. "We saw him watchin' us from that saddleback. Been there all morning. Ma gave me a blueberry pie to bring out to him—kind of a peace offerin'. But when I rode out, he galloped away. A crazy-lookin' devil he was, wearing a red-shirt and breechclout."

"Well, bless me," said the little round woman. "There's no sense in worryin' about that savage now." She beamed at Fargo. "I'm Ma Clemm and this here's my boy, Matthew."

"Name's Fargo," Fargo returned. "Skye Fargo."

"My, what a lovely, poetic name," Ma Clemm exclaimed. She turned to her son. "Ain't that so, Matt?"

"Yup," said her son solemnly, "it sure 'nough is."

By that time the tall man who had stepped out of the barn on Fargo's approach had reached the porch and was joined by a young man carrying a pitchfork.

"Pa! Aaron!" Ma Clemm cried happily. "This here's Skye Fargo. An' he's come to room with us for a spell. Ain't that so, Mr. Fargo?"

"Reckon so. If you've got a room for the night."

Pa Clemm nodded solemnly to Fargo, then removed his hat to wipe off his face and neck with a filthy polka-dot handkerchief. Rawboned, with a lantern jaw, long, scrawny neck, eyes sunken into deep hollows, Pa Clemm resembled an ambulatory skeleton decked out in bib over-

11

alls and clodhoppers. His son Aaron bore a spooky resemblance to his father—only on a larger scale. His outsized, lanky figure rippled with powerful muscles.

"We've got a room, sure enough," replied Pa Clemm. "Hell, we've got more'n one. We got plenty." He grinned suddenly, revealing large black teeth. "Things've been a mite slow."

"They'll pick up, though," said Aaron confidently. "We're expecting a wagon train through here any day now."

"Enough talkin'," cried Ma Clemm happily. "Come in, Mr. Fargo. Get yourself settled. You're just in time for supper, Lord love you." She seemed so delighted at the prospect of his company that for a moment Fargo expected her to clap her hands like a child.

As she turned to go back into the house, a girl about twenty appeared in the doorway and smiled at Fargo. She was a lush-looking armful with dark coils of hair falling down onto her shoulders, clear past the rising plateau of her firm, upthrusting bosom. She had probably been working alongside her mother in the kitchen. There was flour on the front of her apron and a smudge of it on one cheek.

Her dark eyes took Fargo in quickly, and he saw her straighten a bit in the doorway, coming alert the way a poker player does when he finds himself filling an inside straight. There was about this young girl a wet-lipped, tarty loose-ness suggesting to Fargo a damn good time

12

ahead; and though he couldn't be absolutely certain of it, he thought one of her dark, liquid eyes closed in a sly wink.

"This here's Melody," said Matt, grinning.

"Say hello to Mr. Fargo, Melody," said Aaron.

"Hello, Mr. Fargo," said Melody, her voice a husky, teasing lilt.

"You can call me Skye," he told her.

"All right, Skye."

"Here," said Pa, lifting the pinto's reins off the hitch rack, "let Aaron take care of yore hoss, Mr. Fargo. Boy, he's a right purty one. Indian, ain't he?"

"He's an Ovaro pinto," Fargo told him.

"Forages on grass too, I'll bet," said Aaron, his eyes lighting as he took the reins and surveyed the pinto's powerful, chunky frame.

"He does that," Fargo replied, untying his warbag from the saddle and lifting his Sharps from its scabbard. "Comes in handy on long rides."

"I'll bet it does."

Ma Clemm disappeared back into the hotel, but Melody remained, leaning back against the wall, her hands behind her, her bosom and belly thrusting out provocatively. She was wearing slippers and it didn't appear to Fargo she had anything under her thin, tattered dress. She was appraising him coolly, her dark, almond-shaped eyes glancing boldly at his crotch.

"You ridin' alone?" asked Matt.

"Yeah," replied Fargo. "I'm ridin' alone."

13

"You ain't a lawman, are you?"

Fargo was about to tell Matt it was none of his business, but he didn't want to get off on the wrong foot with this family—especially if the two men he wanted were somewhere on the premises.

"Nope," he replied. "But I'm hoping to meet up with a few friends of mine who're staying here."

"Friends of yours, you say?"

Fargo smiled. "That's right. I heard tell they're waiting for that wagon train you mentioned."

"Where'd you hear that?" asked Pa Clemm, sending a black dagger of tobacco juice to the ground.

"The commanding officer back at Fort Larned."

"Well, we did have two such guests," Pa Clemm admitted easily. "Lieutenant Becker weren't lyin' none about that. But them two ain't here no more." He sent another gob of chewing tobacco at the ground. "They already rode out."

"When?" asked Fargo, doing his best to hide his disappointment.

"Near a week ago."

"I thought they were going to wait for the wagon train."

"That's what they said. Guess they got tired of waiting."

"Which way'd they go?"

"West."

Pa grinned suddenly at Fargo, but his eyes were no longer so friendly. "You say you ain't a lawman, but you're sure enough after them two. That right?"

Fargo nodded wearily. "Maybe you could describe them to me. I might have the wrong ones."

"I can describe them," said Melody, walking to the edge of the porch steps and sitting down on the top one. Leaning back on her elbows, she let her knees open slightly and began to describe the two men.

At the end of her description of the two men, Fargo knew for damn certain sure that Melody Clemm was wearing nothing at all under her dress. And her description of the two men was complete enough for him to realize that once again he had arrived too late.

"That's them, all right, Melody," he told her.

"Does this mean you won't be stayin' for the night?" she asked, her knees moving apart a fraction more.

"Doesn't mean anything of the sort," Fargo replied. Tiny beads of perspiration were standing out on his forehead. "I could use a good feed and a good night's sleep. I'll be staying."

Melody smiled and got to her feet. "I'll tell Ma to make dumplin's," she said as she vanished inside.

Pa Clemm joined Fargo as he started up the porch steps. "You'll be wantin' a bath," he said. "We got a room set aside in back of the kitchen.

15

Finest washtubs west of the Mississippi. Had them shipped all the way from St. Louis. There's plenty of hot water and soap, and Melody'll wash your clothes for you too. She'll boil 'em real good."

"I'd appreciate it if you'd tell Aaron to bring up my bedroll so I'll have a change."

"Yessir, I sure will, Mr. Fargo."

The hotel lobby was simply a large living room with a small desk in a corner and a stairwell leading upstairs. The walls had no pictures, none at all. And there were no decorations on shelves or standing in corners on tables. A thin sheen of dust lay over everything.

Pa Clemm moved behind the desk, dipped a metal pen in an inkwell, then turned the register so Fargo could sign. The pages of the register were filthy, their edges yellowed and cracked. Squinting at the last signature, Fargo could barely read it.

He signed the register, after which Pa Clemm, chattering cheerfully, ushered him into the back room. Rusted galvanized tubs were sitting about waiting for use. If they had been shipped all the way from St. Louis, Fargo reflected, that must have been a very long time ago.

Leaving him for a moment, Pa returned to take his clothes, by which time Fargo had stripped down to his long johns. After Pa Clemm left, Melody entered carrying a bucket of steaming water. She smiled quickly at him and proceeded to fill the tub. It took three trips in all. When it was filled, she indicated as much and left the room.

Slightly disappointed, Fargo peeled out of his long johns and stepped into the steaming water. He splashed about for a while, scrubbing himself with abandon. He was about to step out when Melody returned and proceeded to scrub down his back, twice rinsing it with bucketfuls of hot water. Her hands were quick and warm and thorough, and soon the brush she was wielding had peeled off acres of Kansas soil. Then she scrubbed his hair, working the lather thoroughly into it before rinsing it with a stinging bucketful of steaming water.

During all this time, Melody worked so close to him that the warmth of her heavy, billowing breasts gave him a fierce, painful erection. Nevertheless, she made no attempt to follow up the promise of that wink she had flashed at him earlier from the hotel doorway.

Until she was finished.

In the act of wringing out the sponge, she leaned suddenly over and her hand dived into the water. Squeezing his erection in a viselike grip, she kissed him on the lips, her mouth working like something alive. Then, before he could reach up to grab her, she was gone, leaving behind the ghost of a laugh as she closed the door behind her.

"Sakes alive, Mr. Fargo," Ma Clemm cried, her round face beaming. "You ain't hardly scratched

17

that pile of mashed potatoes—and don't forget that pork gravy. If I do say so myself, it's the best I done in a long time."

Smiling, Fargo reached over for the potatoes, but it was Melody, hovering over the table as she helped her mother serve, who got the bowl first and handed it to him. As soon as he had placed it down next to his plate, Matthew was handing him the gravy and Aaron the platter of pork chops. Fargo hurried to fill his plate.

He was on his second helping, and in truth he had never tasted pork chops this good, nor such smooth, delicious mashed potatoes and gravy, not to mention the thick slabs of homemade bread and the rich, golden butter he was in such a hurry to spread on it. But it was the rhubarb pie Fargo was looking forward to, and he was anxious to leave some room for it.

Melody finished helping her mother and sat down beside him. While serving him earlier, she had bent so close her warm, pillowlike breasts had almost pressed against his face and neck. Now, as he pulled over the bowl of pork gravy, Melody edged her chair closer and rubbed her knee against his thigh. It was her bare knee he was feeling, Fargo realized, which meant she had pulled her skirt up past it. Her hand dropped casually to her lap and a second later found its way to his crotch. Fargo almost spilled the gravy over the linen tablecloth.

Melody giggled at his reaction.

Pa Clemm glanced at them. "Looks like you

two young 'uns have hit it off," he said, chuckling. "Saw it first thing. Just you go slow, Mr. Fargo. Hear?"

Forking a pork chop onto his plate, Fargo nodded. He was willing to go as slow as the law allowed. The trouble was, he didn't see how he could fight off this hot she-cat, not the way she was coming after him. After all, he was only human.

Watching Fargo, Matthew nudged his brother as he chomped on a piece of pork, his eyes alight. It was obvious the two brothers knew precisely what Fargo was up against. Abruptly, Melody's hand found its way in under Fargo's pants, and before he could pull away, it closed about his erection. He nearly jumped straight up. As it was, he dropped his fork.

"Now, Melody," cried Ma Clemm fretfully, aware that her daughter was up to no good, "I'd thank you to let our guest eat his supper in peace."

"Aw, Ma," Melody complained, "I was just funnin'."

"You heard Ma," snapped Pa Clemm. "Sit back there now and eat your vittles."

Melody reluctantly pulled back from Fargo and began to eat. Relieved, he reached for another pork chop. But no sooner had his teeth closed about the succulent meat than Melody's hand once again closed about his erection—as if it were a handle she was using to keep him close.

"Lord love you, boy," cried Ma Clemm,

19

placing a platter full of sliced bread down on the table. "You sure got a good healthy appetite. Does a woman good to see food disappear this fast. You want more pork chops?"

So fervently did Ma Clemm speak on this matter that what Fargo realized suddenly was her wig slipped down over her forehead. She snatched at it quickly, planting it back where it belonged. Looking closely for the first time at her round, cheery face, Fargo saw the coarse, wrinkled texture of her skin just beneath the powder and rouge plastered over it.

"No, thanks," Fargo managed. "If I eat another pork chop, I'll likely turn into a pig."

"Well, now, we wouldn't want that," said Matt.

"No, we surely wouldn't—and that's the truth," seconded Aaron.

Melody giggled. "You're too nice just the way you are," she told Fargo, leaning so close she singed him.

Leaning back suddenly, Pa dropped onto his plate a well-gnawed bone. Wiping his hands down the front of his bib overalls, he glanced at his wife. "Ma, how about slicin' me a piece of that rhubarb pie while I go get my jug."

"Now, Pa! There's no sense in going to that jug this soon. Can't you see we got ourselves a visitor?"

"I didn't say he couldn't join me, did I?"

"No, thanks," said Fargo. "I'm stuffed."

"Suit yerself," said Pa, getting up to go after

the jug. He glanced back at Ma. "You heard me, Ma. Cut me a wedge of that pie."

Obediently, Ma Clemm went over to the sideboard and began slicing the pie into quarters. Melody's hand closed about Fargo's rigid shaft and she leaned close to nibble on Fargo's ear, her hot breath searing him.

With a sigh, Fargo gave up any thought of the rhubarb pie, the hot fragrance of which had maddened him the moment Ma Clemm placed it down on the sideboard.

He had another, fiercer appetite to satisfy.

When Fargo finally left the table, Pa was deep in his cups and Melody was over by the sink, washing dishes. Ma Clemm hurried over to him and lit a candle to lead the way upstairs to his room. He mumbled a good night to the Clemm clan. Grinning, Aaron and Matt waved the pork-chop bones on which they were still gnawing. Melody glanced across the kitchen at him, a look of pure raw desire flaming in her cheeks.

Inside his room on the third floor, Ma Clemm put the candle down on the nightstand, turned down the covers for him, then bid him good night and closed the door firmly behind her. Fargo had stripped to his long johns and was relaxing on his back, the candle flickering beside him, when he heard the light, rapid knock on his door.

Not at all surprised, he got up and went to the door and pulled it open. Melody glided in swiftly. He closed the door and turned to her. She flung

21

her arms about his neck and kissed him, holding nothing back.

A second later, his senses reeling, he pushed her away. "Your pa know you're up here?"

"Of course not. He's still nursing that jug and Ma is busy in the kitchen."

"And your brothers?"

"They rode off somewheres. What're you afraid of? Me?"

He smiled at her in some exasperation. "Why wouldn't I be? You almost raped me at the kitchen table."

"It's been such a long time since I seen a man as big as you. I'm just a good healthy woman, is all. Am I too much for you, Mr. Skye Fargo?"

"A man's got to be careful," he told her. "That's all."

"You want me to go on back down to the kitchen?"

Fargo took a deep breath. When the day came he didn't feel up to handling a woman—any woman—he might as well put a bullet through his head. No one could tell what was waiting beyond the next hill, but that sure as hell shouldn't keep a man from riding over it to find out.

He stepped forward, took Melody's face in his hands, and kissed her on the lips harder than she had kissed him. When he finished and stepped back, it was obvious this time it was Melody's senses that were reeling.

She grinned back at him weakly. "Is that your answer?"

"It is."

She plucked at a few buttons, then flung her dress over her head and stood before Fargo stark naked. Her figure was as lush and ripe as a peach at harvest time, with a waist almost narrow enough for him to span with his hands and with hips that flared lushly into thick, powerful thighs. Her pubic patch was as big as a platter and gleamed like a dish of blackberries. Smiling lewdly at him, she moistened her slack, full lips, then shook loose her long dark hair, allowing her curls to tumble clear down past her shoulders, a few of the dark strands coiling about her large, pink areolae.

It was clear he had another feast in store for himself.

Stepping close, Melody stripped off his long johns. Peering at his surging erection, she laughed. Then, pushing him gently but firmly back toward the bed, she fell upon him, fastening her full, pouting lips upon his. Inflamed, he thrust her under him and prowled over her, his powerful muscles rippling like a big cat's, his lake-blue eyes smoldering with need for her. Laughing, Melody reached up and ran her fingers through his thick shock of black hair.

"You got Indian blood, ain't you?" she said.

"On my mother's side."

"Mmm, I knew it. I like that. You won't just roll over afterward and go to sleep."

He fastened his lips around her nipples and felt them swell upward eagerly, becoming as hard as cherry stones. She began to moan. His lips traversed down into the hot, sweaty valley between her snowy mounds, then continued on down to her belly button.

"Go further, Fargo," she pleaded. "Please! Oh, please!"

He obliged. She kicked wildly, plunging her hands through his hair. Grinning, he scooted up onto her. Her great thighs parted eagerly, and he plunged his shaft into her soaking cleft, surging past her outer lips, grinding in recklessly, without caring whether she was ready or not.

She was ready. More than ready. He began thrusting frantically, his need to climax outracing his control. As he slammed into her repeatedly, she laughed and sucked him still deeper inside her, scissoring shut her thighs and flinging her arms around him, cleaving him to her with the strength of barrel staves. Her mouth found his neck just under his ear and her sharp white teeth clamped down, hard. He howled, then laughed, as he came within her triumphantly.

Feeling him come, she bucked happily in response, her entire body shuddering convulsively. Panting, he looked down at her.

"That was for openers," he told her.

"It better be," she told him fiercely.

Pulling out from under him, she turned over on the bed and lifted her rear end, showing him how she wanted it. With a shrug, he obliged.

About an hour later, she was on top of him, slowly gyrating, bringing him to climax. It was amazing how she could keep him going. At last lightning struck his groin and he began plunging and rearing furiously, impaling her upon his fiery sword. Keening aloud, she flung her head back as she came. He filled her with what little he had left while she continued to pulse and gyrate, her hands reaching down to grab his hair while she came again and again. He marveled at her capacity for orgasm and did what he could to keep his erection solid until at last, moaning softly, she flung herself down upon him, tucking her hands under his chest and hugging him gratefully.

A profound lassitude fell over him—as if he had been drugged. Crooning softly, Melody kissed him softly on the lips, gently stroking his damp hair back off his forehead. Abruptly, she thrust her tongue past his slack, unresponsive lips and probed wantonly. But this time Fargo could not respond. She pulled back and Fargo heard her soft, delighted chuckle.

He was only dimly aware of her pushing herself off the bed and pulling the bedclothes up around him, then stealing softly from the room, her dress tucked under her arm. He heard the door close behind her, took a deep breath, and rolled over to face the window.

On the small nightstand behind him, the candle was still burning, its pale, flickering light casting his shadow on the wall beside the shut-tered window. It bothered him. He turned back around to snuff out the candle. Then he remembered something: he was sleeping in a strange bed without a weapon of any kind under his pillow.

This was not how he had managed to keep his scalp for so long.

He groaned, not wanting to move. He was totally exhausted. But a deep, insistent voice chided him for his foolishness. A woman was one thing, but his life—and the search for those remaining two men—was something he could not risk, no matter how tired he was.

Muttering against the effort it took, Fargo pushed himself upright and stared blearily at the corner where he had piled his gear, the Sharps leaning against the wall, his gun belt and six-gun on the floor under it. He pushed himself off the bed and padded woozily over to the corner, slipped his Colt out of the holster, and brought it back to his bed. Dropping onto the mattress, he shoved the big revolver under his pillow and closed his eyes. He was asleep before the mattress stopped moving under him, the candle still glowing on the nightstand beside him.

Like a wild animal, Fargo awoke instantly, every sense alert. That part of him that never slept had heard something: the sound of a board creaking just outside his door. The creaking sound had ceased abruptly, the way it does when the person stepping on the board freezes.

Facing away from the door, his eyes on the wall near the window, Fargo kept himself perfectly still and waited. When the sound did not come again, he began to drop off once more and was almost completely under when the candle's flame flickered sharply, and Fargo saw his shadow wavering on the wall.

Someone had opened the door.

His fingers closing more securely about the Colt's grips, he kept his eyes on the wall. When the door opened all the way, the candle's light danced so violently it almost went out. The flame steadied, and a moment later Fargo heard a floorboard creaking not five feet from his bed as a heavy, stealthy foot eased carefully down upon it. Fargo counted to five, then flung himself completely around, flinging up his Colt as he did so.

He found himself staring into the startled faces of Aaron and Matthew Clemm. Stark-naked, their testicles hanging from their crotches, the two brothers looked like unclean apes, legs bowed, hair wild, their faces livid with the excitement of the hunt—and each one holding in his hand a huge, gleaming hunting knife.

Behind them, guarding the doorway, stood Pa Clemm, his gaunt face alert as he held in his powerful, bony hands what looked like a crowbar.

astonorging that the beam remained in place on the other wall shelter posed in t home to each and the wall of the

2

Kicking out, Fargo flung the two brothers back against the nightstand. The candle toppled to the floor and immediately went out. In the sudden darkness, he rolled off the bed, coming down hard on the wooden floor. The two brothers' shadowy figures loomed above him. He fired up at them. One of them cried out. Answering rifle fire came from Pa Clemm crouched in the doorway, which meant that was not a crowbar he was carrying. Fargo flung himself around and sent two quick shots at Pa Clemm.

"Don't shoot no more, Pa," screamed Aaron. "I'm hit!"

At that the two men stampeded from the room, and a second later the door was slammed shut and the key turned in the lock, after which came the sound of a heavy beam sliding into place across the door. Fargo relit the candle and tried to open the door. When he could not get it to budge, he fired his remaining rounds at the lock, destroying it. But the beam remained in place on the other side, and he could not budge it.

He was trapped.

Or so they thought. Swiftly reloading his revolver, he dressed and went to the window. Peering down between the shutters, he saw figures hurrying across the moonlit yard like frantic insects fleeing a disturbed nest. The Clemms. Then he saw a mounted Indian wearing a red shirt charging across the yard, scattering the Clemms before him. Muzzle flashes lit the darkness, but the Clemms kept going and vanished into the big horse barn.

The Indian was not alone. A white man, smaller in stature than the Indian, raced out on foot from behind the general store and headed across the compound toward the horse barn, his gun drawn. Fargo flung open the shutters to call out to them—and noticed the bars on his window.

Then he smelled the smoke.

Glancing back at the door, he saw the dark tendrils curling up from under it. Glancing back out his window, he saw the growing block of light coming from just under it. Abruptly a searing tongue of flame licked out into the night, sending a shower of sparks up past his window. The Clemms had fired the place!

Grabbing his rifle, Fargo used its stock to shatter the windowpane. He leaned out then and shouted down to the Indian. At the sound of

Fargo's voice, the Indian pulled his horse around and looked up in Fargo's direction.

"Up here," Fargo shouted. "The third floor!"

Shading his eyes, the Indian caught sight of Fargo and waved to indicate he saw him.

"I'm locked in up here," Fargo shouted down.

Riding his horse back to the hotel, the Indian flung himself off his horse and disappeared into the house.

At that moment Fargo heard a sudden flurry of gunfire just as a covered wagon rattled out of the rear of the largest barn, the three Clemm menfolk riding alongside it. As the Clemms fled the compound, the white man who had disappeared into the barn came running out of it, firing after the Clemms. But the wagon and riders had already disappeared into the darkness. A second later one of the smaller barns and the general store erupted into flames. The Clemms, it seemed, were attempting to leave nothing but ashes in their wake.

Fargo went to the door and started kicking at it in an effort to break through the beam holding it. But the harder he kicked, it seemed, the less he was able to accomplish as the smoke, now pouring up steadily from under the doorframe, increased in intensity. Eventually it drove him back and away from the door.

Returning to the window, he tried to rip out the bars with his bare hands, but the bars were firmly secured into the window frame. Meanwhile, the broken windowpane had caused a draft that was now sucking the smoke into the room in greater and greater volume. His eyes began to water, and he could feel the floorboards under his feet warming up. He looked down at the yard and saw the Indian run from the hotel.

A safe distance from the hotel, the Indian turned and glanced up at Fargo. "Fire too much," he called. "No can get upstairs!"

"Throw up a rope," Fargo called.

The Indian ran over to his mount, unlimbered his reata, and tossed one end of it up to the window. Reaching out through the broken windowpane, Fargo lunged at it, but missed. The Indian tied a small chunk of wood to the end of the rope, whirled it around his head a couple of times, then sent the weighted rope up a second time. Fargo managed to grab the reata and hauled it into the room. Looping it around the bars on the window, he tied it securely and waved to the Indian.

The Indian, joined now by his white companion, snubbed the reata around his saddle horn and urged his mount away from the hotel. The bars squealed in protest as they were pulled free of the window frame. The Indian then untied the reata from the bars and galloped closer to the blazing hotel, flinging the rope up to Fargo again. Leaning far out of the window, Fargo caught the reata, hauled it into the room, and tied it to the bedpost, then dragged the bed over to the window.

Glancing down, he saw the rear of the large

horsebarn burst into flames and thought at once of his pinto. With the stock of his Sharps, he smashed out the window's remaining sash, then tossed down his warbag, saddlebag, and bedroll. Testing the reata with a couple of quick pulls, he climbed out the window with his Sharps slung over his shoulder, and swung down the side of the building. Kicking himself away from the flames eating upward toward him, he landed on a portion of the balcony still untouched by the flames, and dropped to the ground.

As soon as he landed, he released the reata and darted across the compound toward the horse barn.

"My horse," he cried to them.

They understood at once and followed in after him. The pinto was stamping impatiently in his stall. Slapping on his saddle blanket and saddle, Fargo grabbed the pinto's reins hanging on a nail beside the stall, slipped on the halter, and led the pinto out through the smoke. Meanwhile, the white man and his Indian companion were busy leading the other horses out, after which they set them loping toward the meadow, well away from the terrifying smell of smoke.

As Fargo picked up the gear he had thrown from the window and finished saddling his pinto, the Indian and his white companion busied themselves releasing the rest of the livestock milling in the corrals. Then the white man went for his own horse, which he had tethered behind the supply shed.

By that time the three men were surrounded by blazing buildings that were rapidly turning night into day.

"Let's get the hell out of here," Fargo shouted above the roaring flames.

There was no need for discussion, and a moment later the three men spurred from the compound and kept going until it was safe enough to pull up and look back. For a while they watched the blazing inferno in silence.

Then Fargo turned to the Indian. "I owe you my life," he said to him.

The Indian shrugged, his dark face impassive.

"Who're you?" the Indian's companion asked. He was a small, wiry fellow, with dark eyes and hair, his round face tanned to a nut brown. He looked as tough as hickory wood. Fargo had noted how high he rode on his horse, like a jockey, and that he was a superb horseman. His left cheek was swollen with chewing tobacco, and he packed a Walker Colt and a Hawken, the Walker almost as long as his thigh.

"Skye Fargo's the name," Fargo replied. "I thought I was going to spend a quiet night under that hotel's sheets for a change. And who might you be?"

"I'm Jim Barrows, and this here's my sidekick, Red Shirt. Go easy. He speaks better English than I do, and he's a whole lot smarter."

"I'll remember that," said Fargo, shaking Jim Barrows' hand, but not shaking Red Shirt's. Fargo knew that Indians did not like the white man's custom of constantly shaking hands, considering it a foolish, unclean habit.

"You're a lucky man, Fargo," Barrows said. "Most guests of the Clemms never do get to see the next day."

Abruptly the flames burst through a hole in the hotel's roof, sending a shower of blazing cinders into the air. For a moment the three men watched this spectacular tongue of fire as it leapt through the night sky.

"Who started the fire?" Fargo asked.

"The Clemms."

"That's what I thought. They did it just to kill me?"

"Hell, you shot one of them, and I guess that messed up their plans some. But it could have been Red Shirt's appearance. Ma Clemm caught sight of him and spread the alarm. This is the way the Clemms usually leave a place—in flames."

"Why?"

"To wipe out any evidence they might have left behind."

"Evidence of what?"

"Tomorrow," Jim Barrows said wearily, "I'll show you tomorrow."

Red Shirt said, "We sleep on the ground." He grinned at Fargo. "No sheets tonight, I think."

Fargo nodded back at the Indian. "That will suit me just fine."

The next morning, still around the campfire,

they were joined by a small delegation from Fort Larned, a Corporal Welch and two privates, sent by Lieutenant Becker to see if he or his men could offer any assistance. The watch at the fort had seen the glow in the sky the night before and the C.O. had realized at once from the glow's direction that the Clemms' hotel was on fire.

The three soldiers were in time to join Fargo and the others in a cup of coffee while they looked over the still-smoking ruin left by the Clemms. The supply shed was the only building that had survived the fire that destroyed the hotel, the general store, and the barns.

The coffee gone, they mounted up, Barrows leading the way to the supply shed.

"What the hell're you expectin' to find?" asked the corporal.

"Remains."

"Of what?"

"I won't have to explain anything once you see for yourself."

Skirting the still-burning barns, they pulled to a halt behind the supply shed. There were signs of digging in the area, recent digging. Everywhere about him Fargo saw the small, ragged holes in the prairie turf, with white, rootlike remnants visible in the shallow diggings.

"Who done this digging?" the sergeant asked.

"I did," said Barrows, "last night. I only had a small shovel, and no pickax." Barrows and his men dismounted. Crowding around him, they watched as Barrows took his small shovel from

the pack behind his saddle and turned over the
loose sod from one shallow grave, then bent and
pulled into view the remains of a bone—a long
bone.

"This here is the remains of a guest at the
hotel," Barrows said. "And he did not die a natu-
ral death."

The corporal frowned. "You sure of that?"

"Look closer. This poor son of a bitch had been
wounded badly in the thigh. You can see where
the bone had splintered from the bullet—and
here, where it was shattered by a blow, from a
rifle butt more than likely.

"My God," said the corporal, his voice hushed.

"There's other graves—all through here," Barrows said, gesturing around him. "The remains
of men, women, and children. Some of the bones
aren't as clean as this one. The worms ain't had
much of a chance to get at them yet. Dig anywhere around here and this's what you'll find."

"You saying the Clemms did this?" Fargo
asked.

Barrows looked at him and nodded curtly. "I'll
explain later. Now let's go inside this shed."

They went around to the front and found the
door still padlocked. Barrows shot the lock off,
then pulled the heavy doors open. A couple of
lanterns were found hanging from nails alongside the door. Barrows and Red Shirt lit them,
revealing a dark, burnt-out hole in the floor, a
huddle of rags to one side of it that smelled
sharply of kerosene.

"I got in here in time to put out this fire," Barrows explained. "Otherwise this supply shed would have gone up like the others."

Then he led them through the neatly piled boxes of farm implements, flour barrels, and other provisions. He was looking for something, and seemed disappointed at not finding it.

"What're you looking for?" Fargo asked.

"A huge steamer trunk. It was in here yesterday. While Red Shirt was drawing their attention, I slipped into here to look around. I guess they must have managed to take it with them, after all."

"What was in it?"

"Their loot. The rings, the gold and silver coins, the bracelets and jewelry they took from their guests after they killed them."

The soldiers exchanged glances, their faces registering the horror they felt. Maybe some of them, Fargo realized, had at one time or another visited the hotel, grateful for Ma's cooking and Melody's warm bosom.

At last Barrows gave up searching for the trunk.

"It's not here," he said. "No question. They must've got suspicious when they saw Red Shirt earlier in the day and loaded it onto their wagon after supper."

"Let's get the hell out of here," said the corporal, his voice hushed.

There was no argument to that as the six men tramped out of the supply shed.

*　　*　　*

At Fort Larned, in Lieutenant Becker's office, Jim Barrows told his story to the commanding officer, Fargo sipping bourbon in a chair off to one side while he listened.

According to Barrows, the Clemms hailed from Springfield, Massachusetts, where, until five or six years ago, they ran a small, hardscrabble farm. Losing their shirt finally, they packed their belongings in a small Conestoga and took off for the West.

" 'Course, that wasn't the only reason they lit out," Barrows said, plunking a gob of chewing tobacco in the brass spittoon by the lieutenant's desk. "Seems like they weren't much liked in Springfield. Nothin' anyone could put their fingers on, mind you, but bad things seemed to happen when the Clemms were around, and an alarming number of people—men, women, and children—kept disappearing. It was like they had a kind of dark zone around them, and whoever stumbled into it vanished."

"So they were driven out of Massachusetts," Fargo suggested.

"More like they were not encouraged to stay, and since they'd dried up all their credit, they had nowhere to go but west."

The lieutenant chuckled ironically. "And these are the hardy souls who are about to tame the land, the settlers we plead for to fill up the West."

Becker was pulling on a pipe. His light hair

38

was cut close, his tanned, lean face handsome, his alert eyes dark brown. To one side of the lieutenant's desk sat Red Shirt.

"Settlers not tame this land," he told the lieutenant. "They destroy it. They cut down the trees, dig up the grass, and dig holes with little houses over them and fill the holes with shit."

"You won't get any argument from me on that, Red Shirt," said the lieutenant. "I agree heartily." The lieutenant turned his attention back to Barrows. "Go on, Barrows. If the Clemms came from Massachusetts, how did you learn of them?"

"My brother Ed and I had a small spread in Texas along the Gulf Coast, near Danford. These here Clemms took over a rundown hotel in Danford on the trail leading to the border, and pretty soon they got a reputation for real fine hospitality and ample servings at their table. And every free male and some not so free wanted to get into their daughter—and not a soul was turned away. Any man who winked at her hit the jackpot."

"I've seen the girl," said the lieutenant, pulling reflectively on his pipe. "A wild, lovely thing, with a devil in her eye."

"Anyway," continued Barrows, "one spring I left my brother in charge of the ranch while I drove some cattle to Louisiana. When I got back, my brother had disappeared. It was as if the ground had swallowed him. I asked around everywhere, but no one seemed to know what had happened to him. Finally in Danford, I ran across a friend who said he had seen my brother visiting with Melody Clemm on their hotel porch."

"He'd been seeing her before, had he?" Fargo asked.

"This was the first time I knew of him visitin' her."

"So you went to visit the Clemms."

"Yes. They remembered Ed. And Melody was most solicitous. They had no idea where Ed had gone after he left their hotel, but they wanted me to stay the night with them. They seemed really concerned about me and convinced me I should not have to ride all that distance back to the ranch alone. What I needed, they said, was a good night's sleep."

"So you obliged."

"I sure as hell did. And it was some meal they fed me, I must admit." Barrows shook his head and took a deep breath. "I wasn't in my bed more'n a few minutes and there came this tap on my door and Melody spilled into my room to spend the night. I was in no mood to resist, I can tell you."

Barrows paused, and not a man in the room uttered a sound.

Clearing his throat, Barrows continued. "That night, after a pretty exhausting session with Melody, they came for me. But I had suspected something from the beginning. They just seemed so damned anxious to have me to stay. So I guess you could say I was ready for them. When they entered my room and rushed me, I had my gun out before they reached my bed and managed to wound the old man, and with one swipe of my right hand managed to rip most of Ma Clemm's hair off her head. When they realized they wasn't goin' to have an easy time with me, they rushed out and tried to lock me in the bedroom, but I broke free and took after them. One of their sons got off a lucky shot, wounding me pretty bad. I was lucky to be able to get out of there."

"So now they knew the cat was out of the bag," suggested Fargo.

"Right. The night I broke out of the hotel it was set ablaze and the Clemms fled the town. 'Course, I still didn't know what in hell them crazy bastards was up to. So when I was strong enough to move around, I searched the ruined hotel and the grounds around it. Then I began digging and found a body. Then the townsmen joined me. It was like this morning, Fargo. Everywhere we dug, we found the remains of those who had once stayed overnight with the Clemms—and then stayed a hell of a lot longer. When this came out, people in town began remembering old acquaintances who had disappeared or lonely travelers who had passed through on their way south and never been heard of again."

"Jesus," said the lieutenant softly.

Jim Barrows nodded solemnly. "In a near empty chest in the cellar of the hotel, we found a few trinkets and valuables belongin' to those they had murdered." Barrows lifted his hand, revealing a large gold ring with the Circle B brand stamped on its face. "In the bottom of that chest I found this ring. My brother was wearing it when he disappeared."

There was a brief silence after that, broken at last by the lieutenant. Turning to the Indian, he asked, "What about you, Red Shirt?"

The Indian spoke up then. "My brother's scalp was found in same trunk. Already I been in town many weeks to find my brother."

"You had reason to believe he was in Danford?"

"Yes. He tell me he go find Clemms."

"Why?"

"He search for family who murder our mother's people. These whites, they ride up in covered wagon to my mother's lodge beside Washita where she make camp. Three men and two white squaws. They stay night, and when they leave, everyone in lodge and in rest of small encampment dead. Only one girl live to tell of them. She hurt bad, but she crawl away into shallows to escape their knives. They take much jerky and other food. Big snow come then and we cannot follow."

The lieutenant shook his head in wonderment. Fargo felt the same icy sense of horror. These Clemms were like a traveling plague.

"What can I do to help?" the lieutenant asked.

Jim Barrows spoke up. "Send out scouts to ask about the Clemms at every town and village. I figure they're heading west toward Colorado, but I can't be sure."

"And we'll need warrants of some kind," said Fargo. "And you're the only law out here, it looks like."

"You are joining in the hunt for this family, too?"

"Yes. I have to find out what happened to those two men I had tracked to their hotel."

The lieutenant nodded decisively. "You'll get whatever official documents you'll need to bring in these devils. We've had a lot of desertions this past six months or so—and now that I think of it, everyone of them were poor bastards eager to visit that dark-haired vixen at the hotel."

"Melody Clemm," said Fargo softly.

"Yes. Jesus, what a name for a creature like that."

Fargo nodded and leaned back in his chair, recalling what it was like making love to Melody. For a tantalizing instant he felt again her lips moving over his face and neck and could smell the hot, musky perfume of her ripe body, hear again the soft murmur that came from her like the purr of a silken cat. She was not a beautiful woman, or if she was, Fargo hadn't noticed, for that was not the explanation of her power over men. It was in the way she looked at a man, the full ripeness of her body, her almost searing warmth when she pulled a man close—the aching, sensual music of her.

For this temptress, Melody was the perfect name.

3

When the lieutenant's patrols returned to Fort Larned, they reported that the Clemms had last been seen in Spring Creek, on the Colorado border. They had left Spring Creek talking about making South Pass before the snows caught them. The Clemms had impressed the local townsmen by spending prodigiously on supplies and wagons. On hearing this, Barrows nodded grimly, remembering that steamer trunk filled with gold coins and other valuables the Clemms had managed to take with them.

Fargo and his two companions rode into Warlock, Colorado, not long after. Winter was hovering over the town like a fist waiting to descend. Warlock was about a hundred miles north of Spring Creek, high in the Rockies, sitting alongside the trail that cut north to South Pass. It was dusk as the three men rode down Main Street past the Warlock Hotel, a building of four stories that appeared to have been freshly painted.

44

Glancing at the building in passing, Fargo found himself staring at a familiar young lady in the act of shaking a dust mop out of a second-floor window. Melody Clemm. Their eyes met. Pulling in the mop swiftly, she slammed down the window.

"Did you see what I saw?" Fargo asked Barrows and Red Shirt.

"We saw," Barrows replied, his small, round face grim. "Looks like they gave up the idea of getting through the pass before winter."

"I not think we sleep in that hotel," said Red Shirt, his black eyes gleaming at Fargo. "But maybe you want to give her a kiss hello, Fargo?"

"Not right now," Fargo said as they continued down Main Street. "But if we're going to make a move on them, we better do it fast. Melody sure as hell knows what we're doing here."

They found a smaller hotel on the other end of town and left their horses in a livery across the street from it. The hotel's desk clerk was a kid about sixteen. He took one look at Red Shirt and dived behind the desk, coming up with a Greener.

"Put down that cannon, sonny," Fargo told him, reaching across the desk and slamming the barrel down, "or I'll cut your liver out!"

"But he's a redskin! He ain't allowed in here!"

"He's with us. He's allowed."

"What is all this?" demanded a sharp woman's voice.

They turned to see a tall, attractive woman of

thirty or so striding toward them from the hotel's dining room. She was wearing a pale pink dress that just brushed the carpet; her bosom was full, her neck long and graceful.

Then she saw Red Shirt.

"Oh," she said, her dark eyes flicking quickly over the handsome savage. "An aborigine!"

"No, I am Cherokee," Red Shirt asserted proudly.

"He's with us," said Fargo, "and we want rooms."

"Of course. But may I offer you a word of advice?"

"What is it?" asked Barrows.

"Get Mr. Cherokee into a pair of Levi's. A coat and hat wouldn't hurt, either. He'd get by then without any trouble and be welcome in my saloon and restaurant."

"Good idea," said Fargo. He turned to Red Shirt. "You mind wearing Levi's and a coat, Red Shirt?"

The Indian smiled, his wide, powerful face showing no resentment at all. "It will soon be cold in this high country. White man's pants and coat will be much warmer, I think."

Fargo turned back to the woman. "Ma'am, you got any idea where we can fix him up this late?"

She laughed. "Follow me."

In her private office she selected a pair of Levi's and a long black frock coat, the only one in her wardrobe closet capable of fitting over Red Shirt's impressive shoulders. Stepping behind a screen, he pulled on the pants, then slipped into the frock coat. Then the woman found a tan, low-crowned plainsman hat for him. Red Shirt stepped out from behind the screen and placed the hat carefully on his head, grinning. The hat pleased him, it seemed, most of all.

"How much do we owe you?" asked Barrows.

"Nothing," the woman replied. "Chalk it up to Warlock hospitality."

"This your hotel?" Fargo asked her.

"Yes. My name is Jan Sheridan, and you can introduce yourselves by signing the register." She smiled quickly. "And now I must get back to my other guests."

They followed her out of the office and registered.

That evening they ate a hearty meal in the hotel's restaurant, then entered the adjoining saloon. They found the place surprisingly empty. Fargo was disappointed. He had hoped for a smoky, crowded place ringing with the clamor of drinking, gambling men. And maybe a little brawl or two. Such play loosened a man up a bit.

The bar girls outnumbered the patrons and were dressed in provocatively short dresses with plenty of spangles. Before long, Barrows was dancing with one of them—if two people clutching clumsily at each other and jumping up and down in place is dancing. They made a somewhat comical couple, since Barrows was not much taller than the girl, and what few patrons were in the place laughed and stomped their feet whenever Barrows and the girl got too close. For his part, Fargo waved away a couple of bar girls, and none of them seemed willing to sit on Red Shirt's lap. It was probably the fierce, hungry gleam in the Indian's eyes that kept them away.

As Fargo sipped his beer alongside Red Shirt, he tried to figure his next move. They had found the Clemms. Their best course now would be to approach the town constable first thing in the morning—or the county sheriff if he was nearby—and seek his aid in apprehending the Clemms. Fargo had all the necessary papers, and if that didn't work, they would simply take them back to Fort Larned without the help of any local lawmen.

Only, the thing was the Clemms knew Fargo was in town, and they would sure as hell be likely to make a move of their own before . . .

"You some kind of Injun lover, you son of a bitch?"

Fargo looked up, startled. He had been so deep in his own thoughts he hadn't noticed the burly gent looming over the table.

Fargo put down his stein. "You speaking to me, mister?"

"Yer damn right I am."

Fargo grinned up at the man's long-jawed, stupid face. "What's your problem?"

"You—and this here redskin," the asshole blustered. "What d'you mean bringin' him into a place where white men drink?"

"He's my friend. He goes where I go."

"That so?"

"Yes," said Fargo happily as he pushed himself away from the table and stood up to face Long Jaw. "And maybe you'd like to do something about it."

Fargo noticed that the big ape challenging him was not armed. So if the stupid son of a bitch wanted to mix it up, that was all right with Fargo. He dropped his gun belt.

Long Jaw picked up a chair and brought it down on Fargo's head as hard as he could. Fargo warded off the chair with his left forearm and swung his own chair from the side, driving the big man sideways into another table. As Long Jaw went down amid a shower of crunching chairs, Fargo leapt over his table and landed on him. His big hands closing about Long Jaw's neck, he began thumping the big fellow's head on the floor, rapping it so sharply the man's eyes began to roll back into his head. Intent on finishing him off, Fargo hauled Long Jaw upright and sent a series of slashing lefts and rights to his face and midsection. The big galoot remained on his feet, however, swaying like a big tree about to crash to the forest floor.

Abruptly, a strong hand grabbed Fargo's shoulder and spun him around. Before Fargo could haul up his hand to protect himself, a huge fist crunched into his face and sent him reeling back. This new assailant was bigger than Long Jaw, and as Fargo straightened up to punch the fellow, a revived Long Jaw grabbed Fargo from behind and pinned his arms.

With a cheerful snarl, the second man charged in and began punching Fargo in the head and face with powerful, pistonlike shots. That was when Barrows joined the fray. Letting loose with a war cry that rattled the timbers, the little man leapt through the air and came down on the back of the one punching Fargo. Like an infuriated monkey, he wrapped his forearm around the fellow's neck and yanked back with sudden, cruel force. Pulling up frantically, the big man reached up and began clawing frantically at Barrow's forearm. Unable to free himself, he began spinning around frantically in an effort to throw Barrows off his back, but the grinning Barrows hung on.

Fargo spun around to finish off Long Jaw. Backing up fearfully, the big fellow flung up his forearms to ward off Fargo's attack. Thoroughly aroused by this time, Fargo battered through Long Jaw's feeble defense, driving him relentlessly back until Fargo had him right where he wanted him: flat against a wall with no place to run. Calmly and deliberately Fargo sent a quick series of punches to the man's face and jaw, battering him mercilessly until at last he collapsed loosely to the floor.

Fargo stepped back, panting heavily, his head buzzing. Only then did he notice that his own nose had been spread over his face, a steady flow of blood oozing from it. He swiped at the flow clumsily, then forgot about it as he turned to see about his other assailant.

He needn't have worried. The fellow was on his knees, plucking weakly at Barrow's forearm, which had closed like a vise about his windpipe. Every now and then Barrows would loosen his grip long enough to enable the man to gulp in some air, then he would swiftly tighten it again. It looked as if the little man's brown forearm had grown into the man's neck.

Behind Barrows, sitting in a chair with his back to the wall was Red Shirt. There was a Colt in his hand and an unconscious man sprawled at his feet. The Colt was trained on the barkeeps and the saloon's patrons. It was Red Shirt's gun that had convinced them to keep their distance.

"Let the son of a bitch loose, Jim," Fargo told Barrows.

Barrows leapt off the man's back. The big fellow sagged forward onto his hands and knees and looked dazedly around. Fargo hauled him upright and settled his hash with one punch, a pile driver to the chin. The fellow was unconscious before he hit the floor. Flopping over, he lay on his back in the sawdust and, to the amusement of everyone watching, began to snore.

Fargo stepped back and held a handkerchief up to his nose as Jan Sheridan rushed into the place just ahead of the bar girl who had gone to get her.

"Gentlemen," she cried, "what is the meaning of this?"

The saloon quieted instantly as everyone

turned to face her. It was her oldest barkeep who spoke up. "Bullhead and Tim went after them three over there," he said, indicating Fargo and his two companions.

"Why? What did they do?"

"Hell, they brought a redskin in with them and it riled Bullhead."

Jan walked over to the two men sprawled unconscious on the floor. Pushing aside the shattered chairs, she stared contemptuously down at them, then over at the man Red Shirt had evidently taken the Colt from. The fellow was conscious now.

He stared blearily up at her and grinned. "Hi, Jan."

"What about you, Ace?" she asked.

Ace shrugged and rubbed his head gingerly. "Guess I stuck my head in where it didn't belong."

"I'm glad you realize that. This Indian and his two companions are my guests at this hotel. Get out of here!"

Ace shrugged and got to his feet. Red Shirt handed the man his Colt. Mumbling something and holding on to his head, Ace dropped the gun into his holster and left the saloon.

"Sam!" Jan Sheridan called.

A swamper pushed himself through the gaping crowd.

"Get rid of Bullhead and Tim," she told him. "Dump them out back, alongside the privy. Maybe the smell will bring them around."

Dropping his bucket and mop, the swamper grabbed both of Long Jaw's feet. A barkeep hurried over and reached down for the one called Tim. Others joined them and in a moment the two unconscious men were gone.

As the patrons returned to their drinks, the girl Barrows had been dancing with earlier led him back out onto the sawdust floor to continue their jumping and pawing. With a weary sigh, Jan Sheridan brushed a lock of hair out of her eyes and sat down at the table where Fargo and Red Shirt were now sitting quietly. Fargo was pressing a handkerchief over his nose.

"I'm very sorry this happened, gentlemen," Jan told them. "People in town are nervous about Indians. The Washo and the Utes've been causing trouble in the area."

"I'm sorry about the broken furniture," said Fargo.

She smiled. "It is of no consequence. It's a long time since this place has been active enough for a good brawl."

"Who were those two men?" Fargo asked.

"Bullhead Johnson and Tim Walters. Two no-accounts. You probably knocked some sense into them."

"Join us in a drink?" Fargo asked.

"Thank you," she replied graciously, pulling a chair over and sitting down. Taking a closer look at his face, she said, "You might have a broken nose there."

He shrugged. "Maybe."

Turning in her seat, Jan Sheridan waved over a barkeep and sent him to find some ice and water and towels. As soon as they were brought, the entire saloon was treated to the spectacle of Jan Sheridan placing cold packs on Fargo's nose to stem the bleeding.

She did fine, her hands quick and efficient, and before long Fargo was drinking beer once again, his bloody, swollen proboscis throbbing only slightly. One of the bar girls, a dark-eyed lass with more than a little Indian blood, approached Red Shirt, and the big Indian didn't protest at all as the girl pulled him off to an empty table.

Fargo glanced around at the near-empty saloon. The brawl should have brought in half the town to watch, but the place was still needing customers.

"Your business seems to be down," he remarked.

"Yes," she said. "Way down."

"Competition?"

She nodded. "A new saloon in town."

"Next to the Warlock Hotel, maybe."

"Yes."

"And run by the Clemms."

"You know them?"

Fargo shrugged. "I'll give you all the details later. How long they been in town?"

"Long enough to make a hotel dining room appealing. I'll say that for them. Nothing fancy, but heaping portions of good food, all at prices so low anyone would be a fool not to eat there. Same with the saloon. The drinks are cheap, but good. I don't know how they can afford to do it, but they're running me into the ground."

"And of course they've got quite an attraction."

"You mean Melody Clemm."

Fargo nodded.

"You know her, do you?"

Fargo grinned. "A most fetching young lady."

"That's what half the men in this town have been saying since she arrived. Something tells me you know a whole lot about this lady and her family."

"It's a long story."

"Then why don't we finish it somewhere else?"

Somewhere else turned out to be just where Fargo had hoped: Jan Sheridan's apartment. She led him to her bedroom, pushed him down gently on her bed, and told him to relax. A basin of warm, soapy water was brought. Loosening the bun of auburn hair on her head, she let it cascade down her back. Then, leaning close, she gently bathed his nose, then the rest of his face and head. As she leaned close, Fargo noted how heavy and dark her brows were, and how long her lashes.

Finished with his face, Jan peeled off his clothes and gave him a complete bath from head to toe, taking special pains at certain strategic sights. Not to be outdone, Fargo returned the favor. When the mutual laving was completed,

Jan lowered herself slowly on top of him, her long, sinewy frame covering his neatly.

She kissed his face, then his nose—lightly. "I don't think your nose is broken after all," she told him.

"It's a pretty tough nose."

"You said you were going to tell me about the Clemms."

"Not now."

She nibbled at his earlobe. "All right."

She kissed him on his lips, softly, tenderly, her lips probing his as deliberately as if she were tasting a delicate fruit. He was already more than ready for her, and suddenly, without warning, she adjusted her body ever so slightly—and like magic his shaft slipped into her warm, moist sheath, penetrating it to its furthest depths.

"Ahhh . . ." she sighed, her arms enclosing him.

He started to turn her over, but she held him back. "No," she said. "Stay where you are and try not to move." She smiled then, her teeth gleaming in the dimly lit bedroom. "Just try not to move. See how long you can do that."

He put his arms around her and kissed her—as softly and as tenderly as she had kissed him. Soon, though he tried to keep himself from thrusting as she had suggested, he pressed his hand down onto her buttocks and began to press upward slowly, subtly. Then she too began to move in answer to his thrusts, pressing down on him, inducing a slow, seductive rhythm that increased only slightly in intensity. He felt the sweat standing out on his body. His erection was on fire as it slowly, ever so slowly pressed deeper and deeper into her, while the muscles inside her vagina clasped him ever more tightly, working his foreskin back and forth, like a lubricious hand.

He was soon on fire. He began to groan. She brushed the perspiration off his forehead and kissed him on the eyelids, then let her lips brush his. They were on fire. With a sudden, delicious wantonness, she thrust her tongue into his mouth. The fire in his loins exploded. With an angry, infuriated growl, he flung her over on the bed, his hand still on her buttocks, and slammed her up into him. On his knees straddling her, he thrust wildly for a short while and exploded deep within her—just as she too, laughing delightedly, came as well.

Clasping each other tightly, they continued to convulse until at last, so weary his head was spinning, Fargo rolled off, still panting, and growled at her, "Where the hell did you learn that trick?"

"A fantastic Frenchman."

"I won't ask the circumstances."

"As you have probably guessed, I was not always the owner of a hotel."

"What were you?"

"The wife of a French count."

"Then you are a countess?"

"I was."

"But you're not French. You're an American."

She wrinkled her nose. "It shows, does it? But you're right. I was brought up in Philadelphia. My parents shipped me to Europe to continue my education, as they called it. What they were hoping for was that I would find myself a wealthy husband, since so many of the men I had been seeing had little or no social standing. You can imagine how delighted my parents were when I wrote them that I was engaged to marry a French count."

"So what are you doing here? And where's the count?"

"I'm doing my best to survive. This hotel, which poor Phillipe won in a card game, is all he was able to leave me when he died."

"I'm sorry."

"Don't be. It was a foolish death."

"How so?"

"A duel. A matter of honor, Phillipe called it. He insisted on a duel with all the trappings. But the other fellow did not believe in waiting until the full count before pulling the trigger. My gallant, honorable husband did, however—and died with two bullets in his chest."

"Why the duel? Was it over you?"

"Don't be silly. Phillipe had more sense than that. The other man was a gambler. When he lost to Phillipe, he accused Phillipe of cheating."

Fargo shook his head. What a damn fool way to go! A formal duel with a seasoned gunslick because the man had accused him of cheating.

58

The gunslick must still be laughing. "What happened to the gambler?"

"I shot him with Phillipe's gun."

"Jesus. *You* killed him?"

"Of course. He killed Phillipe, didn't he?"

Fargo's surprise gave way to soft, appreciative laughter. The gunslick was not still laughing, then. Fargo drew Jan closer to him. He was getting to like this French countess more every minute.

"By the way," he said, "Sheridan doesn't sound very French."

"I took my maiden name back. No one out here could spell my husband's name."

"What were the two of you doing out here, anyway?"

"His family fortunes were in decline, as Phillipe put it. Of course, he had told me nothing of this during our courtship—and when my parents heard how much of a decline, they refused to help."

"So he came west to find his fame and fortune."

"Yes. Precisely. You have no idea the fanciful tales that have swept Europe since the discovery of gold in California. Of course, Phillipe believed every bit of it, and with all that gold strewn upon the ground from here clear to California, it seemed a simple thing to hurry over with his young bride and recoup his fortune. He was sure it would not take longer than a few months."

Fargo nodded. Since the forty-niners, this foolish story had been told and retold throughout the West. Men, desperate to recoup fortunes or make them, abandoned everything they had in the fool hope that all they would have to do was turn over the soil to pocket a fortune.

Her hand dropped to his crotch. "You want me to do it your way now?" she asked.

"Hell, there was nothing wrong with yours."

"I know it," she said, kissing the dark coil of hair on his chest. "But variety really *is* the spice of life."

With that, her lips traveled to his belly, lingered there for a while, then kept going—all the way. His fingers reached into her hair as he guided her. Her hands fondled him roughly for a moment before her hot lips closed about him teasingly. He moaned. Laughing softly, she released his shaft and let her lips move back up his belly.

Fargo moved into position. She laughed at his eagerness and scooted up, turning onto her back and spreading her thighs. For a moment he ducked his head down, his tongue scalding her muff; then he plunged his shaft deep into her. This time they did not fool around. He was on fire, bucking like a randy goat.

Only seconds from his climax, Jan called out gleefully, "That's it, Fargo! Fuck me!"

And he did.

It was the next morning, at the breakfast table in Jan's apartment and after the dishes had been cleared away, that Fargo told Jan about the Clemms.

"Do you suppose," she asked when he had finished, "that they're robbing and killing their customers now?" Her voice was hushed.

"No. Not now. All they're interested in now is keeping their head down and building up their clientele. They've got enough treasure in that trunk of theirs to give them a real edge when it comes to underselling their competitors."

"I've noticed," Jan said glumly. "Fargo, you've got to do something."

"That's why we're here. Tell me about the law in this town."

"We've got a county sheriff right down the street. Sheriff Beaman."

"What's he worth?"

"I heard my barkeep say he wasn't worth a bucket of warm spit. I'd agree."

"I'll go see him anyway. The Clemms know Jim and I are in town, so they must be up to something already."

"Then go see Beaman now."

Fargo finished his coffee, then got up.

Jan walked with him to the door of her apartment, gave him a bold, provocative kiss, then pushed him out the door before he could retaliate.

"Now let me get this straight," said Sheriff Beaman, leaning back in his swivel chair, his head cocked. "You three are telling me that if I

61

don't watch out, the Clemms are gonna start killin' and robbin' their guests. That it?''

"That's what we mean, Sheriff," insisted Barrows.

Fargo was standing in front of Beaman's desk with Barrows and Red Shirt on either side of him. The sheriff was a very big man with shoulders wider than any Fargo had ever seen. The only thing wider was his stomach, which flowed out over his gun belt like an oversized batch of bread dough. The sheriff's features were squeezed into a small area of his puffy face, his eyes barely visible as bright, deep-set raisins.

The sheriff's two deputies had filed in after them and were sitting now in wooden chairs under the gun racks. They had turned around their chairs and were leaning on their backs, studying Fargo and his two companions intently, as if they had been expecting the three men's arrival and were waiting for them to hang themselves.

Beaman cocked an eye at his deputies, then glared back at the three men standing before him. "Proof," he said. "Let's see proof."

Barrows shrugged. "You'll just have to take our word for it."

"You got a warrant? Dodgers?"

"It's on your desk in front of you," Fargo said. "It's all there in that statement from the Fort Larned C.O."

Beaman reached down and flung the paper back across his desk at them. "A pack of lies," he sneered contemptuously. "Fool, crazy lies. I can't believe you three would march in here and spill out such bilge, and expect me to believe it. Though maybe I ain't all that surprised. I was told you'd be in here with this kind of crazy talk."

"By the Clemms," Fargo said.

"Yes! By Melody. I mean, Miss Melody Clemm."

"Gotten to know her, have you, Sheriff?"

"Yes, I have. She's a right sweet young lady. Not only that, but I got reason to believe she's gonna be Missus Beaman before long."

"When did she give you that idea, last night?"

The man's doughy face went purple. "I don't see that's any business of yours."

"Sheriff," Barrows said, interrupting him almost gently, "are you willing to take this chance? Suppose what we say is true?"

"But it ain't, damn you," the sheriff cried, pushing himself erect and glowering furiously across his desk at them. "I call these lies you been spreadin' vicious slander. If I needed it, that'd be another reason for me to put you three under arrest."

"Arrest?" Barrows demanded. "You can't do that!"

The sheriff smiled triumphantly and flung the warrant toward them across the desk. "Sure I can. For assault and battery. And I got witnesses."

"You talkin' about them two men who went

after us in the saloon last night?" Barrows asked, incredulous.

The sheriff nodded emphatically. "That's right. Tim Walters is in a bad way. If he dies, the charge'll be murder. We may be only a small village in the middle of nowhere, but I'm the law in this here county and I ain't goin' to let two no-account drifters and a redskin get away with terrorizin' my town!"

"You're full of shit, Beaman," said Fargo. "This is a frame, and you know it."

The sheriff turned to his deputies. "Take 'em!"

The deputies stood up casually, drawn Colts gleaming in their hands. Smiling, they advanced on the three and disarmed them, then pushed them around and marched them into the cell block. A moment later Fargo was staring disgustedly out through his cell's barred windows, Barrows beside him, while a very unhappy Red Shirt began pacing in the adjoining cell.

They were locked securely away, and Melody Clemm's new boyfriend had the keys.

4

It was a smirking Melody Clemm who visited their cells to bring them their dinner meal, and then their supper. After each visit she lingered a while with the sheriff, and they could hear his delighted chuckles as Melody entertained him. When she left the last time, Fargo turned and stared out through the bars at the deepening black night and swore.

"I hear you clear," muttered Barrows, relaxing on his bunk. "We got to get the hell out of here."

Red Shirt was sitting on the corner of his bunk, staring through the bars at Fargo and Barrows. "I have plan."

Fargo turned to him. "I'm listening."

"After I get down on floor, shout," Red Shirt told them. "Shout loud. When sheriff or deputies come in, you say I stab myself. Say no Indian can stand to live behind bars. All white men believe this."

Fargo and Barrows exchanged glances. "What the hell," said Fargo. "It won't hurt to try."

Barrows nodded. "Go ahead, Red Shirt. Get down on the floor."

As soon as Red Shirt got down, the two men began calling loudly to the sheriff. He didn't show, but his two deputies did.

"What the hell's the matter?" the first one demanded.

Fargo pointed to Red Shirt. "He's stabbed himself. There's no redskin that can stand being cooped up in a white man's jail! You ought to know that."

"Shit," said the deputy, producing a key and swinging open the cell door.

As he and his companion stepped into his cell, Red Shirt sprang to his feet. With one massive blow from his right fist, he staggered the first deputy, grabbing his holstered sidearm before the man hit the floor. But as he swung around to take on the second deputy, this worthy brought the barrel of his Colt down on top of Red Shirt's head.

Red Shirt's knees buckled, but he somehow managed to stay on his feet and tried to shake off the blow. The deputy brought the gun barrel down a second time. Slowly, Red Shirt collapsed to the floor. The first deputy staggered back up onto his feet, delivered a few well-aimed kicks to the unconscious Indian's torso, then followed his companion woozily from the cell.

As the second deputy locked Red Shirt's cell,

he glanced over at Fargo and Barrows. "Don't worry. You won't be locked up much longer. You'll be tried first thing in the mornin', and I'm thinkin' it won't be long after that when you all start dancin' on the end of a rope."

"You must be crazy," Barrows shot back.

"A trial?" Fargo demanded. "What for?"

"That feller you punched out yesterday, Tim Walters, he died this afternoon. Ma Clemm did all she could to save him, but there was nothin' she could do. Ma and Pa Clemm's seeing to the funeral right now, and they've closed their saloon out of respect. They loved Tim like a son."

Without further explanation, the two deputies filed out of the cell block and closed the door behind him.

Fargo eased down onto his bunk and stared at Barrows.

Barrows shook his head. "It don't look so good, Fargo."

"I know it doesn't. We're fighting the whole damn town. The Clemms've used that trunk full of gold and silver to buy every damn fool in this place."

"Yep," said Barrows, staring through the bars at the unconscious Red Shirt. "And, by Jesus, it's workin'."

A gloating Sheriff Beaman stopped in not long after to confirm the news of Tim Walters' death, and about an hour later Fargo had another visitor: Jan Sheridan. She looked as beautiful as ever, but quite subdued in manner as she came to a halt outside Fargo's cell.

"You heard?" she asked Fargo.

"We heard."

"You're being framed. Tim was not badly hurt. The swamper who helped drag him out of my saloon said he was sleeping peacefully with his back against the privy the last time he saw him."

Fargo nodded glumly. "I figure the Clemms killed him."

"I agree," said Jan.

"But that don't matter, though, does it?" said a grim Jim Barrows. "Not a soul in this town would believe it."

Jan shook her head in wonder. "You're right. The town's gone mad. The Clemm family seems to have taken over the place. Anyone says a bad word against them is in trouble."

Fargo grinned ironically at her. "Money talks."

"When's the trial?" Jim asked.

"Tomorrow. One of the deputies has already ridden out for the circuit judge."

"We won't have a chance."

"You won't if you mention anything bad about the Clemms," Jan agreed.

"Jan," Fargo said, "I think maybe you better get us out of here."

She looked at him for a long moment. "What do you think I'm doing here?" She reached into her bosom and pulled out of her ample cleft a double-barreled derringer.

As Fargo reached through the bars to take it, he asked, "Can this be traced back to you?"

She shook her head. "No one in town knows I own it. I took it from a gambler some time ago and kept it hidden. Will it be enough for you?"

Fargo examined it. It was fully loaded. "It'll be fine," he told her. "Just fine. Now get out of here. We won't try anything until well past midnight. Can you get our mounts in the livery saddled and ready to go by that time?"

"Yes. And I'll take your gear from your rooms and have them on the horses, too."

"Thanks, Jan."

She looked at him for a long moment, then moved closer to the bars and pressed her face against them. As he kissed her, she smiled impishly. "And I thank *you*, Skye Fargo."

Then she was gone.

"I can see the dipper," Barrows said, craning his neck to see out the window.

"How much moonlight?" Fargo asked, cocking his derringer.

"Not much."

"How you feelin', Red Shirt?"

"My head, it sing sad song. I get that man. I take his head off, I think."

"Just stay on the bunk and groan, like I said."

Red Shirt nodded, lay back on his bunk. The sound of his groaning wail filled the cell block.

Trouble was, since he was an Indian, Fargo couldn't tell if he was singing or moaning. He waited a few minutes, then leaned his shoulder against the bars and called out, "Hey! Deputy! Get in here!"

Fargo heard a cot squeak in the next room, then heavy feet hitting the wooden floor. A moment later the door to the cell block was flung open and the deputy that had played a tune on Red Shirt's noggin poked his head into the cell block. His hair was wild, his eyes unfocused. He was a very tired, groggy man.

"What the hell's all this racket?" he demanded, scratching his head.

"Red Shirt's dying. He's havin' convulsions. You hit him too hard on the head, you son of a bitch! Look at the poor bastard."

The deputy peered through bleary eyes at Red Shirt. Red Shirt began to twitch. The deputy's expression did not change. "How do I know it ain't another trick?"

"You remember how hard you hit him, don't you?"

"Mebbe so. But whatta you want me to do?"

"Get a doc!"

"I can't leave you men unguarded."

"Then tell your buddy to get help!"

"He ain't here."

Red Shirt's groans increased.

"Dammit!" cried Fargo. "Get the sheriff!"

The deputy grinned. "Oh, now, I couldn't do that. He's with his sweety, Miss Melody."

"Look at that Indian," Fargo cried, pointing. "Look what you did!"

Red Shirt groaned even louder, and as the deputy stepped finally into the cell block and approached Red Shirt's cell, Red Shirt's twitching grew terrible to see.

The deputy was more than impressed. He peered in at Red Shirt, his eyes wide. "Jesus Christ," he said, "he's havin' a fit, sure enough."

Red Shirt began to moan louder. Jim Barrows clasped the bars and peered into Red Shirt's cell, concern writ large on his round face.

Peering into the Indian's cell, the deputy backed toward Fargo's cell. "How long's he been like this?" he asked Fargo.

"Since a little after supper," said Barrows, peering sorrowfully in at his twitching friend.

"Well, I ain't goin' into his cell," the deputy said. "Sheriff Beaman said he'd have my badge if I did."

"Well, we have to do something," Fargo said. "Neither of us can sleep with him carrying on like that."

"How about I douse him with a bucketful of water?"

"Through the bars, you mean?"

"Yeah."

"That might help."

But before the deputy could carry out his scheme, Fargo reached through the bars and tapped the man on the shoulder. When he turned

71

to face Fargo, he found himself staring into a derringer's twin bores. The deputy lost his color.

"You take a step back or call for help and I'll kill you," Fargo advised him. "We have nothing to lose, the way we look at it. You know what I mean?"

"Sure. Just go easy!"

"Then open up these doors and let us out of here."

"Sure. Sure thing. . . ."

The deputy unlocked both cell doors and groaned slightly when he saw Red Shirt rise from his bunk, his dark face impassive. Pulling the deputy's Colt from his holster, Red Shirt crunched the barrel down onto the deputy's head. The deputy dropped like a sack of potatoes. Stepping over the deputy's body, Red Shirt followed Fargo and Barrows out of the cell block into the sheriff's office.

They found their weapons and gun belts and helped themselves to a few boxes of cartridges. They left by the rear door, keeping to the back alleys until they reached the livery stable. Entering it, they found their horses already saddled, their gear secured to the cantles, just as Jan Sheridan had promised.

Ducking their heads, the three men clattered swiftly out of the barn, galloped down the dark Main Street and out of town.

From a crag high above the town, the three fugitives watched as the town came alive about fifteen minutes later. It was the deputy raised the alarm as he rushed from the sheriff's office, screaming his fool head off. The windows in the town began to show light as people woke to complain of the noise. Before long the sheriff, pulling on his frock coat, his bulk making him impossible to miss in the dim light, hurried from the Clemms' hotel to his office.

A crowd soon gathered in front of the jail and from its members a posse was formed. There was a lot of shouting and some protesting at the choices made by the sheriff, but before long Beaman led his posse at full gallop out of town, heading north, following the same trail Fargo and his companions had taken not long before. In this dim, moonless night, however, Fargo was confident the posse would never cut their sign, and even if they did, there was no way they would catch the spot where Fargo and his two companions had left the trail and doubled back.

The three men waited until the clatter of the posse's hooves had died completely and the town had gone back to sleep before they angled down the steep slope toward the Clemms' hotel. Keeping to the back alleys, they rode through the town, emerging at last behind the hotel. They dismounted under a clump of cottonwoods and proceeded the rest of the way on foot.

Fargo was the first through the rear door. In front of him was a narrow hallway. Proceeding along it, he passed a laundry room, storeroom, and a door leading to the cellar. He was moving past it toward the kitchen, gun drawn, when he heard voices coming from the cellar. He held up and turned around. From the look on their faces, Red Shirt and Barrows had heard the voices also.

Red Shirt was the closest to the cellar door. He opened it a crack and slipped through, Barrows and Fargo following. Halfway down the cellar stairs, Red Shirt held up and crouched on the steps, his revolver gleaming in the dim light. Crouching behind him, the three men saw the Clemms huddled around a table, a kerosene lantern hanging from a beam over their heads. So intent were they on their discussion, not one of them glanced up at the stairs.

". . . . we got no choice," Matthew Clemm was saying, angrily brushing his lank hair back off his forehead. "That fool sheriff ain't goin' to find them three. We got to move on."

"But we just got settled in real nice," said Melody.

"My land, yes," seconded Ma Clemm. "An' it's so nice here, with everyone thinkin' we some kind of royalty."

"How long you think we can keep that up?" growled Pa Clemm. "That ain't a bottomless trunk, you know."

"Hell, Pa," said Aaron, grinning, "we'll start fillin' it soon enough."

"Don't you see, Aaron?" Matt grumbled. "After what Fargo told the sheriff, we can't do that no more. Anyone disappears, right away they'll start rememberin' what Fargo said."

"So that settles it," said Pa Clemm, slapping his hand down on the table. "We got to move on—and the sooner the better. Winter'll be settin' in before long."

"Cheer up, Melody," said Matt, patting Melody's hand. "Now you won't have to marry the sheriff."

"You didn't really think I would, did you?"

"There's a lot of man there."

Melody popped her brother on the head.

"Stop it, you two," said Pa Clemm. "We got to figure which way we go now."

"The South Pass," said Aaron.

"Yes," repeated Matt eagerly, "and then California."

"Or maybe Oregon," said Pa Clemm.

"We'll put it to a vote," said Ma Clemm. "I hear there's lots of travelers in California."

There was some chatter after that before Pa Clemm quieted them and the vote was taken. California it was. Everyone around the table perked up. It meant a long journey over snowy peaks, but they were game.

Fargo poked Barrows, then straightened up on the stairway and spoke sharply to the Clemms below him. "Keep your hands on the table, all of you! You're covered!" As he spoke, he cocked his six-gun, its ominous click echoing throughout the cellar.

The five at the table froze, their hands in plain sight. Red Shirt darted down the stairs and was the first to reach the table, Barrows right behind him. As the two relieved Pa Clemm and his sons of their sidearms and knives, Fargo descended the cellar stairs, still covering them carefully.

It was Pa Clemm who first spoke to Fargo. "You better get out of town fast, mister. When the sheriff comes back with that posse, you three won't have a chance."

"We'll be gone by then." Fargo smiled. "All of us."

"How's that?" demanded Aaron.

"Means you're moving out, just like you decided. Only you're not going without us and you sure as hell not going to California."

"Where you taking us?" Pa Clemm demanded.

"Back to Kansas, to Fort Larned. There's enough evidence back there to make every one of you swing twice."

"Skye!" Melody cried. "You wouldn't!"

"Why not?"

"Because . . . we mean so much to each other." Fargo looked at her and laughed.

5

When dawn broke, they were well south of Warlock, Pa and Ma Clemm driving the lead wagon,
Matthew and Aaron driving the second and third
wagons. Melody rode in the first wagon with her
parents.

In the lead wagon with Pa and Ma and Melody
Clemm was the huge steamer trunk filled with
the Clemms' grisly wealth. Fargo wanted it for
the evidence it provided, the Clemms for the
wealth it contained. Despite the damning finger
it pointed at each member of the family, not a
single Clemm protested when Fargo told them to
load it onto the wagon. The thought of leaving
their wealth behind for others to spend was too
much for the Clemms to contemplate—at least
not while there was still a chance they might
somehow slip out of Fargo's grasp and take the
trunk with them.

The fourth night on the trail, while they were

still high in the mountains, the Clemms made their first move.

Fargo, having just completed the first watch, was sitting on his saddle, pulling off his boots, when he heard soft footsteps just behind him. Dropping his boot, he turned his head, his Colt already in his hand.

"Hello, Skye," Melody said.

Fargo's first glance was at Melody's hands to make sure they were empty. They were. She was dressed only in a low-cut nightgown cut off a few inches above the knees. More of her was visible than was covered.

"Hello, Melody," he replied, dropping his Colt back into his holster.

She sat down cross-legged beside him, not bothering to push her abbreviated gown down into her lap. "What's the matter, Skye? You been actin' so distant these past few days," she said, her eyes gleaming seductively.

"You mean you don't know?"

"Skye, whatever the rest of the family's been doin' is no concern of mine."

"I see. You've had nothing to do with any of it."

"That's right," she said eagerly. "I'm so glad you understand."

He looked at her for a long moment, wondering if she could possibly be serious. Then, with a shrug, he pulled off his other boot and rolled into his sugan.

Immediately Melody pulled her nightdress

over her head and flung it away into the night. As naked as a plucked chicken, she flung herself into the sugan with him, pulling the covers over them both. He could feel the heat of her body—those of her great, melonlike breasts especially—as she snuggled close against him, her educated hand already reaching for his manhood.

With a sigh, he capitulated, moving over onto her as she opened her thighs, his sudden erection slipping into her moist cavern with ridiculous ease. She giggled softly, and he felt the hot, moist muscles of her vagina closing firmly about his shaft.

Without preliminaries, he began stroking, and before long she was panting and swinging her head back and forth, her tongue running across her upper lip as she bucked eagerly under him, her breasts jiggling and slapping softly in the night. Soon he had pushed himself up onto his knees, driving harder and harder, grinding down into her with a merciless urgency. Abruptly, she came, flinging her hands about his neck, her pelvis lunging up at him, tiny cries breaking from her throat.

"Oh, God," she muttered fiercely after she finished coming, "it's been so long! So long!"

"Shhh," Fargo murmured angrily as he kept pounding, his knees digging into the ground under the sugan.

She laughed and clung to him, doing her best to meet his thrusts. There was nothing fancy about it now as he pounded his way to an orgasm that had him panting weakly at the end of it. After he expended every last ounce of his seed into her, he eased back off her.

Her eyes opened and she stared up at him, grinning lasciviously, "Hell, you ain't done yet," she told him. "We just got started."

Reaching down, she grabbed at him, uttering a tiny cry of disappointment when she found out how much he had lost in the past few moments.

"Sorry," he told her. "It's been a long day for me."

"But you said you had Indian blood!"

"Even Indians get tired."

"Not the ones I've laid," she retorted angrily. "Skye Fargo, you're holding out on me!"

"I'm tired."

"Not *that* tired, surely."

"Go on back to your wagon," Fargo told her.

She slapped him—and would have slapped him again if he hadn't grabbed her wrist. She tried to pull free, but he hung on. It was while the two were struggling that Fargo heard the sound of a foot behind him. He tried to turn, but with a sudden, triumphant smile, Melody pulled free of his grasp and pulled him onto her, exposing his back to whoever was coming at him from behind.

He rolled over swiftly onto Melody, glancing back in time to see Aaron's hand sweep down, the long blade of his skinning knife flashing in the night. The blade took a tiny nick out of Fargo's left shoulder.

"Get back, Melody," Aaron snarled. "Let me at him!"

Melody released Fargo and rolled out from under him as Aaron came at Fargo a second time. Reaching up, Fargo caught Aaron's right wrist with both hands, then sprang to his feet, dragging the startled Aaron after him. Bracing himself, he flung Aaron around with such force that the man's feet left the ground and he slammed headlong into a tree.

As Aaron crumpled, unconscious, to the ground, Fargo snatched up Aaron's knife and turned just in time to catch the full force of Melody's rush as she fell upon him, her fingers hooked like claws. Slashing at his face with the fury of a trapped wildcat, she seemed bent on taking out his eyes—or worse. Fargo hunched his head down, shifted his feet slightly, then brought his fist around in a swift roundhouse, catching her on the point of her chin. She went flying awkwardly and landed on her back. She tried to get up, then rolled over and remained on the ground, whimpering, one hand held to her jaw.

Fargo turned to look back at the wagons. As he had expected, the rest of the Clemms were crouched in the darkness behind the nearest wagon, ready to spring, long knives gleaming in their hands.

"I wouldn't do that if I were you," Fargo told them. "Look behind you."

They did. Barrows and Red Shirt stepped out of the shadows. Barrows had his rifle cocked and ready, Red Shirt his Colt.

"Drop them knives," Barrows growled.

The Clemms dropped their weapons and straightened wearily. Darting in swiftly, Barrows and Red Shirt snatched up their knives and flung them into the night.

Fargo smiled. He had been waiting for this opportunity to flush out what weapons he was certain the Clemms had stashed away. Those knives would have made terrible weapons if the Clemms had been able to use them at close quarters.

Two days later Matthew Clemm slugged Barrows and lit out, taking Barrows' rifle with him. They were in high, rocky country by that time, and it didn't take long for Matt to vanish in the rocks above the trail. An hour later, as the wagons were moving through a narrow canyon, he began firing on Fargo and Red Shirt from a ridge high above the trail.

Dismounting swiftly, Fargo ordered Ma Clemm to pull the wagons to a halt under a rocky overhang. He left the still-woozy Barrows to guard the Clemms, then he and Red Shirt scrambled up the steep canyon side after Matt. Rounding an outcropping halfway up, Fargo was forced to duck low as Matt sent a slug whining off the rock inches over his head. Fargo sent a couple of quick shots into the pine-clad ridge before ducking back.

"I saw his rifle flash," Fargo told Red Shirt. "He's to the right of that clump of pine. Go around. I'll keep him busy."

Red Shirt grunted and set off.

Fargo waited a decent interval, then charged up the slope, keeping his tail down, using the mountainside as a shield as he kept moving toward the ridge. Crossing an exposed stretch of ground, Matt fired on him again, the bullet biting the ground out from under his boot. He went down, clutched at a bush, then dragged himself up through a break in the rocks. He was close enough to the ridge to glimpse the tops of the pines. Pulling himself up onto a moss-covered ledge, he waited for the blast of Matt's rifle.

When it didn't come, he took a deep breath, darted across the ridge and into the pines. Inside the pines, he turned and raced toward the spot where he had seen the flash from Matt's rifle. Too late, he heard Matt crash through a clump of brush right beside him, grunting in exertion.

Fargo spun about in time to see Matt bringing down his empty rifle barrel. Flinging up his forearm, Fargo tried to ward off the blow. He thought he had broken his forearm as he felt himself slamming into the ground. Pulling his Colt, he fired up at Matt. Branches behind Matt disintegrated as the man kicked the Colt out of his hand, then drove the stock of his rifle viciously into Fargo's gut.

Coiling like a stomped worm about the rifle barrel, Fargo attempted to wrest the barrel from Matt's grasp. Matt kicked Fargo in the side repeatedly, slamming him back finally against a tree, the back of Fargo's head hitting it hard.

Fargo lost all control of his movements, let go of the rifle, and stared stupidly up at Matt. The man smiled and reached for Fargo's six-gun. Leveling it at Fargo's forehead, he cocked the weapon.

A sound caused Matt to whirl and fire. Red Shirt showed himself for an instant. Matt fired again. The bullet whined off a tree. Red Shirt darted closer. When Matt fired a third time, the hammer came down on an empty chamber. By this time Fargo had managed to push himself erect. He threw himself at Matt. Matt ducked nimbly aside, flung the empty six-gun to the ground, and disappeared into the pines.

Feeling more than a little rocky, Fargo sank back to the ground, his gut on fire. He was doing his best not to empty his stomach.

Red Shirt bent beside him. "You hit, Fargo?"

"No, just knocked a little silly, that's all."

"Can you get up?"

"I could if the ground would stop moving."

Red Shirt grinned. "I think you got hit in the head too much."

"That's not the only place."

"You want I go after him?"

"Forget him. He doesn't have a weapon. My guess is he'll go back to the wagons now. We'll find him there when we get back."

"Mebbe so. Or mebbe he go on to next town and buy weapons and wait for us."

"He hasn't got the money to buy a pot to piss in. All the money they have is in that trunk."

Red Shirt nodded and sat back on his

haunches, waiting for Fargo to get his wind back. At last, Fargo nodded to Red Shirt, who helped him to his feet. Taking a few steps, Fargo was relieved to discover that his stomach was not going to drop down between his legs. He straightened up. What he felt was not pleasant, but he had suffered through worse.

"Let's get back to the wagons," he said.

Not long after, they were halfway down the mountainside at a point where they should have been able to spot the wagons, when Fargo pulled up, confused.

"Dammit! Where are the wagons?"

Red Shirt said nothing. Instead, he scrambled down another hundred yards or so before pulling up. "They gone," he said.

Fargo came to halt beside him. Like Red Shirt, he saw the tracks leading from under the rocky overhang where he had instructed Ma Clemm to pull the wagons over. But they were gone now. The Clemms must have have overpowered Barrows.

Or worse.

Though they searched the area thoroughly, Fargo and Red Shirt found no sign of Barrows. The Clemms had stampeded their horses and it took them until nightfall to overtake them. Early the next morning, they took after the wagons, and close to sundown the following day, they came to a small hamlet.

When Fargo asked the townspeople about the

Clemms, he found they had passed through there, all right, after purchasing a considerable amount of provisions and weapons from the local general store. Throughout their purchases, the townspeople were quick to note, the Clemms had been most pleasant. They had paid the going rate, no matter how outrageous, with no haggling at all.

When the Clemms left for the South Pass, they took with them a townsman they had hired to help them drive the wagons.

Those who spoke to Fargo expressed the usual interest in the Clemms' seemingly inexhaustible wealth. And more than a few exhibited an interest in their daughter, Melody. The talk about town was that the Clemms had hired the driver not only to handle their horses, but to help them protect their wealth also. The fellow they had hired was a local blacksmith. So taken with Melody was he that he had sold his shop to his apprentice for a ridiculous sum in order to go with the Clemms.

Fargo was not at all surprised.

As he and Red Shirt rode out the next morning, Fargo shook his head and glanced over at Red Shirt. "I'm worried."

"About Barrows?"

"Yes—and that poor fool of a blacksmith."

By late afternoon the two men found themselves riding into the teeth of an early blizzard. It came at them suddenly from over the hills, its first sign a chill wind that seemed to have come from the depths of an enormous root cellar. Behind this chilling wind came a great dark wing of a cloud that plunged the world into a premature darkness. Trailing behind the cloud across the high meadows came what first appeared to be dust, but which soon proved to be snow—heavy, wet stuff coming straight at them with a velocity that caused the flakes to sting them with the force of solid pellets.

They donned their slickers and tried to keep going north, but it soon became clear they would have to find shelter. Turning their mounts, they allowed the animals to move before the wind. Eventually they found a sheltering crowd of rocks and after considerable trouble managed to build themselves a fire and gather what dry firewood they could still find in the vicinity.

For two days they fought the wind and snow and somehow managed to keep the fire going. On the third night first the wind, then the snow let up. They gazed up at a sky resplendent in gleaming stars, tucked themselves deep into their sugans, and slept soundly for the first time since the blizzard hit them.

They awoke to a transformed world. The bright sun flashed off snow so pure they had to fashion crude sunglasses out of wooden twigs they bound together with rawhide. Then they set out once more, pushing through snow that had drifted so deep in places they had to dismount and break a path for their mounts. But it was still October and the sun was bright enough to melt off the snow quickly. In a couple of days there were only patches left, most of them in the pines or in hollows and depressions hidden for most of the day from the direct rays of the sun.

Four days after the blizzard, Fargo and Red Shirt came upon the Clemms. They had just reached the border of one stand of timber and were about to break out of it when Fargo caught the unmistakable gleam of sunlight on white canvas on the far side of the meadow. Pulling up swiftly, he wheeled his pinto back into the timber, then stood up in his stirrups to see the Clemms working to replace a wheel on the second wagon.

"Now what we do?" Red Shirt asked.

Before Fargo could respond, he saw two riders break from the wagons and head across the grass toward them at a hard gallop.

"We've been spotted, looks like."

Red Shirt grunted.

It was Pa Clemm and Aaron. The two were armed to the teeth, shotguns resting across their pommels, six-guns strapped to their sides. The two lean riders looked impressively purposeful as they reined in a few hundred yards in front of Fargo and Red Shirt.

"We been waitin' for you two," Pa Clemm called.

"Give it up, Pa," Fargo told him. "I'm taking you back to Kansas. You're not going to California—or any place else."

"How you gonna stop us?"

"We'll hang back and pick you off, one by one, if need be. You know that. It'll be like shooting ducks in a barrel."

Chuckling, Pa spoke up. "Don't you think we already figured that out?" he grinned wolfishly.

Aaron spoke up then. "We figure we got a way to make you lay off."

"That so?"

"That's right," said Aaron. "We got Barrows. And he's still alive."

Fargo's face hardened, but he gave no reply.

"You follow us any farther or give us any trouble at all, we'll just start taking pieces out of your friend's hide," Aaron continued triumphantly.

"What about that driver you hired? You think he'll stand still for that?"

"Hell, he's already gone," Pa volunteered.

"And Barrows is next," said Aaron. "But he won't go so quick if you two don't turn around and ride back the way you came."

"Hell," said Fargo, "you'll just go ahead and kill Barrows anyway, no matter what we do."

As he spoke, he drew his six-gun, Red Shirt the same. At the distance between them, Fargo reckoned, the shot from the Clemms' shotguns would spread too wide to do them much damage. Fargo started firing rapidly.

Pa Clemm's horse reared, rendering his shotgun useless. Aaron tried to return Fargo's fire, but one of Fargo's bullets slapped into his gun, driving the stock into his shoulder. The gun detonated, the muzzle flash coming so close to the horse's ear that the spooked animal reared in panic, throwing Aaron.

Fargo and Red Shirt turned their mounts and raced back into the timber. Once in its cover, Fargo headed through the woods, hoping to circle around through the timber and come out on the other side of the wagons.

It took Fargo longer than expected, and they were just about to emerge from the timber, guns out and ready, when the first terrible cries came from one of the wagons. It was a long, high scream that ended in a gasp. It was Barrows, his scream like nothing Fargo had ever heard before. The hair on the back of his neck prickled as he brought his pinto to a scrambling halt. Red Shirt pulled up also, his dark, impassive face unnaturally pale. Through a break in the timber, Fargo saw that the broken wheel on the lead wagon had been repaired. The wagons lurched forward.

Fargo nudged his pinto out of the timber and took after them, Red Shirt keeping alongside.

"Get any closer," cried Matthew, leaning out of the rear wagon, "and I'll throw you a piece of your friend!"

As Matthew spoke, Barrow screamed again, this cry even more nerve-shattering than the one before. It sounded as if the man's very soul were being rent from his body.

"All right! All right! We're holding up," cried Fargo. "Leave Barrows alone!"

"Ride off, then!"

Fargo and Red Shirt wheeled their mounts and rode back into the timber. There were no more screams from Barrows, but that did not matter.

In both men's ears, Barrows' soul-shriveling cries still rang.

6

Fargo pushed aside the juniper branches to see more clearly. It was two days later, a little after midnight. The Clemms had formed their wagons into a rough semicircle with a sheer rock wall at their back. Since Fargo and Red Shirt's last encounter with the Clemms, they had gained considerable altitude. At this elevation, the night air was clear and cold, with ghostly patches of snow everywhere. A bright moon sailed overhead.

Fargo turned to Red Shirt crouching beside him. "You go in from the right. I'll come from the other way. I got a hunch Barrows is in that last wagon.

Red Shirt nodded, then ducked back into the pine.

Moving as silently as a shadow, Red Shirt ducked close to the wagon, then stepped up onto one of the traces and peered inside. Something moved in the far corner of the wagon, and Red Shirt saw a pale face turn and stare at him. Peering at him through narrowed eyes, he recognized the face instantly.

Barrows!

Leaping into the wagon, Red Shirt dropped beside him.

"Get . . . out," Barrows croaked painfully. "Dynamite . . . trap! Waiting for you!"

At that moment Red Shirt felt someone rise up behind him. Before he could turn or make any move to protect himself, something heavy and unyielding crashed down upon his head. Without a cry of any sort, he sank into darkness. . . .

Fargo, crouching in the darkness just outside the wagon, heard the slump of a body and boosted himself into the wagon. He was just in time to see a shadowy figure leap out the other side. Then he heard—or felt—a sudden explosion powerful enough to raise the wagon off the ground. A hot shock wave slammed him like a fist. As he went flying back out of the wagon, he heard the sudden thunder of horses' hooves, followed by the crack and rattle of the remaining wagons being whipped into motion.

Fargo hit so hard, the ground knocked the breath out of him. As he struggled to drag air into his lungs, he saw the wagon he had just left was engulfed in flames. Scrambling to his feet, he ran back to the blazing Conestoga. Though the canvas top was ablaze, the bed of the wagon was not yet entirely consumed.

Holding his forearm up to his face to protect himself, Fargo leapt up into the wagon, found the bleeding, broken bodies of both Red Shirt and Barrows, and threw them without ceremony to the ground. Bounding down beside them, he hastily dragged them a safe distance from the blazing wagon.

A moment later Red Shirt was sitting up, rubbing his head. Beside him, however, Barrows remained unconscious. He looked bad. He had been beaten brutally about the face, and one eye was swollen shut. His right arm was twisted out of shape—broken, from the look of it. In addition, he had been stabbed repeatedly in the waist and thigh.

Barrows groaned.

Fargo bent over him. "We got you now, Barrows," he told him. "You'll be all right soon's we get you to a doctor."

Barrows glanced up at Fargo. "A doctor?"

"You heard me."

Barrows licked his dry lips, and the trace of a smile showed on his battered face. "Sure," he said. "Sure . . ." His head sagged to one side and his eyes closed.

Fargo leaned his ear against Barrows' chest. The heart was still beating, faintly but steadily. Fargo got to his feet and looked down at the torn, unconscious body of his friend.

"What we do now?" Red Shirt asked.

"We go find that doctor."

The smell of snow was in the air when they came in sight of Red Gap three days later. The town was huddled at the end of a steep-walled valley, close in under a titanic wall of rock that seemed to reach almost straight up, dwarfing the town and the valley.

They clopped over the plank bridge into the Red Gap. Fargo noticed the unpainted frame buildings, their raw, weathered walls mute testimony to the mean winters commonplace this close to the Continental Divide. The only hotel in the place was a grim two-story affair across from the express office and livery stable. The townspeople saw them riding in, and soon a crowd had gathered to watch them ride down the single main street. Behind Fargo's pinto, strapped to a crude travois, rode Barrows. He was completely out of his head by now, his torn body racked with fever.

Pulling up in front of the barbershop, Fargo dismounted while Red Shirt remained on his horse beside the travois. Entering the shop, Fargo called the barber over to him. The customer he was shaving, his cheeks and jowels frothed with shaving cream, sat up in his chair and stared at Fargo in some irritation.

"There a doctor in this town?" Fargo asked the barber.

"Upstairs. Use the outside stairs. Name's Doc Wilder."

"Thanks."

Fargo left the barbershop, went around the side of the building, and climbed the wooden stairs. His knock was answered by a tall figure in a black frock coat. There was a neat string tie knotted at his throat, a black stetson on his head. Though obviously dressed as fashionably as he could manage, there was an air of desperation about him, as if he were trying very hard to keep up appearances—and failing.

"Yes, what is it, my good man?" he inquired wearily. "The toothache?"

"It ain't me. It's a friend of mine downstairs."

"What's the matter with him?"

"You might have to take off his arm, and he's been cut up pretty bad. Right now he's got the fever pretty bad."

Dr. Wilder's face paled with concern. "Then bring him up here, by all means! I'll go see to his cot!"

An hour later, a thoroughly weary Dr. Wilder stepped softly from the room where Barrows lay on a narrow army cot, unconscious. Fargo and Red Shirt got to their feet. The doctor closed the door and shook his head.

"Was it Indians did this?" he asked.

"No. Worse. Whites."

"I believe you. Who are they?"

"They call themselves the Clemms."

The doctor shook his head in weary disgust.

"Will Barrows be all right, Doc?"

"The arm was broken so severely, I may have

to amputate later. But it is those knife wounds I am worried about. They have become septic. That's what causes the fever. I've cleaned the wounds with whiskey and cut out what dead tissue I could. My hope now is that I got all of it. If I did, he will live. If not . . ." The man shrugged.

"Tell you what, Doc," said Fargo. "Let's not think that way. He's gone through a lot and we'd like him to be alive when we catch the bastards responsible."

The doctor smiled weakly. "I can promise you nothing. But you have my word that I will do all in my power to save him. By the way, there were burns on him as well. His eyebrows are almost completely singed off."

"The bastards that sliced him tried to blow up him and Red Shirt with dynamite they planted under his wagon."

"What terrible people!"

"Mebbe they here now in your town," Red Shirt said.

"I sincerely hope not."

"You look like you could use a drink, Doc," said Fargo.

The doctor's weary eyes gained some spark. "Would you gentlemen be buying?"

"We would," replied Fargo.

"As a matter of fact, I was on my way over to the saloon when you arrived. As soon as I get someone to watch over our patient, I shall join you."

"We'll see you then," said Fargo. He didn't

97

know about Red Shirt, but after watching the doctor work over poor Barrow's torn body, he needed a drink himself. A good stiff one.

A burly customer objected when Red Shirt entered the saloon with Fargo. He was sputtering angrily about dirty redskins and half-breeds when Fargo grabbed the neck of his shirt, twisted it until the man's eyes began to bug, then rammed his boot so far up the man's ass that he went windmilling out through the batwings and crashed through the hitch rack.

That bit of housecleaning accomplished, Fargo surveyed the room and asked if anyone else objected to his good friend's presence in the saloon. There were no takers. The bar's patrons looked quickly away from Fargo's angry, lake-blue eyes and hunched over their drinks.

A moment later Doc Wilder joined them at a table. "Let's have it," he said, "the entire unwholesome story. This remarkable family might someday find their way into my memoirs."

"Memoirs?"

"It is a way I have of passing the long, long hours in this tiny backwater, sir. My way of hanging on to my sanity, you might say. I doubt if these memoirs will ever see the light of day. They are only a comfort for my weary soul. But do go on. Please. I am most anxious to hear about these Clemms."

Fargo nodded and launched into his tale.

When he had finished, Wilder leaned back in

his chair and filled his glass for the third time. Throwing the bourbon quickly down, he fixed Fargo and Red Shirt with brooding eyes. "The trouble," he said slowly and distinctly, "is that I have no difficulty at all in believing you."

"That's so?" Fargo replied.

"Of all the creatures that walk, fly, or crawl over the face of this earth, mankind is, by far, the most ruinous, the most depraved—a jackal has more heart, an ape more dignity, a ravening lion more courage. Why do you think I spend my days in this mean place high among the shimmering peaks of the Great Divide if not to get away from the crowded cities of man, from his noisome prowl, his filthy leavings."

"Well," replied Fargo reasonably, "you sure as hell ain't all that distant from it yet."

Wilder nodded grimly. "As your terrible story tells me only so well, I am afraid you are right. Thank God I never had occasion to take a room for the night from such depraved innkeepers." He slapped his empty glass down onto the table.

"Another drink?" Fargo suggested.

"No," Doc Wilder said, getting to his feet. "I am anxious to see to my patient. By the way, if you're looking for a place to spend the night, I suggest you avoid the hotel. You will find yourself sleeping with very small, unwanted guests. Your best bet is the rooming house at the other end of town run by the widow Shellabarger."

"Thanks."

"You'll find her a good cook, her beds clean,

and"—he glanced at Red Shirt—"she has no prejudices against native Americans."

Fargo watched the doc hurry from the saloon. Earlier, when Fargo was upstairs in the doctor's office, he had glanced beyond it into the doctor's apartment and had glimpsed one complete wall covered with bookshelves, each shelf solid with books.

Doc Wilder was a scholar, no doubt of that. Many of the words he used Fargo was not all that familiar with, but the man was no snob and Fargo liked him. His skill and firm gentleness while tending to Barrows had been a comfort to watch. Unlike most doctors who infested the West, this one had obviously not obtained his degree through the mail.

Fargo picked up the bottle of bourbon and filled first Red Shirt's glass, then his own.

"Hey!" someone near the door shouted. "Here she comes!"

Fargo glanced out the window. A shifting curtain of snow was blowing down the narrow street and the wind was beginning to howl.

Another blizzard.

The widow Shellabarger was a handsome woman in her late thirties with a pile of chestnut hair on her head, a narrow waist, a full chest, and dark-brown eyes as searching as a hawk's. She was all business and didn't bat an eye as she led Red Shirt and Fargo to a large room at the rear of her rooming house. It was complete with a wood stove in one corner. The linen, folded on the end of the bed, was immaculate, the floors and windows spotless, the dresser more than ample for their things.

"How long do you gentlemen think you'll be staying in Red Gap?" the widow asked, her voice friendly.

"We've got a friend up in the doc's office," Fargo replied. "He's pretty sick. I reckon we won't be going anywhere until he's better."

"I see," she said. "Well, your friend is in excellent hands, I assure you. All of us in Red Gap are proud to have a man of such profound learning and compassion as Doctor Wilder in our midst."

Her sudden, fulsome praise of the doctor was so enthusiastic, she blushed.

"He's a fine doctor, all right," agreed Fargo.

"Supper will be within the hour," she told Fargo, reaching back for the doorknob. "You're welcome to join the others in the living room until then. Meanwhile, I'll send my boy in with some firewood."

"Thank you, ma'am," Fargo said.

She pulled the door shut and Fargo glanced at Red Shirt, who didn't look happy. "What's the matter?" Fargo asked.

"I not like sleeping inside under roof. It is not safe, I think."

"Don't worry. It won't come down on you."

"You sure? Look out window."

Fargo did. The howling wind was whipping the street into a white caldron.

Later, when the widow Shellabarger's son, a wiry, towheaded boy about ten years old, came upstairs with the kindling, the room had become chilly enough for them to dig blankets out of their bedrolls and throw them over themselves.

After supper they slogged through three-foot drifts to Dr. Wilder's office to see how Barrows was doing. He was still fighting a fever, but he looked a little better to Fargo, if not to Red Shirt. Wilder, preoccupied, refused to give any prognosis, and to Fargo he seemed quite worried.

Later, while Fargo and Red Shirt were nursing their drinks in the saloon, the doctor entered. Glancing unhappily over at them, he paused long enough to stomp the snow off his boots, then came over to their table and slumped grimly into a chair beside them. There was no glass for him, so he drank straight from the bottle, taking two healthy belts. Then he slammed the bourbon down on the table and glared with sudden misery at the two men.

"Your friend is dead," he told them.

Fargo had expected this announcement from the moment Doc Wilder entered the saloon. "When?"

"Not five minutes ago. I'm sorry, gentlemen. I did all I could. But the sepsis had spread throughout his body by the time he arrived here. If I could have seen him sooner, he might have had a chance. To tell you the truth, it's amazing that little man lasted as long as he did."

Fargo looked at Red Shirt. "Soon as this blizzard lifts, we'll go after the Clemms."

Red Shirt nodded.

Two days later, with the blizzard showing no signs of abating and Red Shirt out somewhere prowling restlessly through the snow, there was a light knock on Fargo's door. Despite the fire in the wood stove, he was standing by the frosted windowpane with a blanket thrown over his shoulders.

"Come in," he called.

Melody Clemm entered. A shawl was thrown over her head and shoulders, and she was wearing a light jacket. Closing the door, she leaned back against it, studying him gravely. "It's warmer downstairs in my room," she told him.

Before Fargo could reply, Melody took a small .38-caliber revolver from her pocket.

"Downstairs," she told him.

"Where we going?"

She smiled. "Not far. My room is in the back."

Melody opened the door for him, and without a word, Fargo preceded her out of his room and down the back stairs.

7

Melody opened the door to her room. Waggling her gun barrel at him, she waved Fargo in ahead of her. In her lamp's dim light, Fargo saw Doc Wilder sitting on the bed. He was slumped forward, his hands folded before him, his eyes downcast. As Fargo entered, Wilder looked up. On his cheekbones were raw, thickening welts caused by Melody's gun barrel. Apparently, she had given him a fierce going-over. Melody closed the door behind her.

"What's all this?" Fargo demanded of Melody. "And where in blazes did you come from?"

"We were almost through the South Pass. But the storm drove us back. When the doc here told me where you was stayin', I took this room."

"What do you want?"

"One of her brothers is hurt, Fargo," Wilder explained. "She wants me to help him, save him if I can."

"What's wrong with the son of a bitch?" Fargo asked her.

"That explosion," said Melody. "The dynamite went off before it should. Matt got flung under our wagon. He was hurt bad and he's gettin' worse. We need this doctor. But damn your eyes, you were here ahead of us—tellin' him more lies about us."

"From your description of her," explained Wilder, "I had some idea who she was the moment she entered my office, and when she mentioned her brother's name, I knew for sure."

Melody leaned close to Wilder. "Were you, now?" she asked, kissing him with wanton boldness full on his lips. "And am I really so terrible?" She stepped back and smiled down at him. "You don't really believe all those lies Fargo told you."

"Of course I believe what Fargo told me. I helped him bury the man your family mutilated."

"Does that mean you won't come with me? You won't help my brother?"

Wilder stirred uncomfortably under her gaze. "I'm a doctor, sworn to help any who need me. But I'll not raise a hand to save the likes of you and your family."

Melody's face hardened into something cold and evil. Still covering both men with her revolver, she flung open the closet door, reached in, and dragged out the widow Shellabarger's boy. He was bound and gagged, the ropes biting cruelly into his young body. As Melody flung him roughly down at Fargo's feet, he struggled weakly, staring up first at Melody, then at Fargo and Wilder. His eyes were wide with terror.

"If you won't come, Doc," Melody said, "I'll take the boy back with me. We'll hang him high and let the wind turn him to ice. He won't thaw out until next spring."

"Do that and we'll come after you," promised Fargo.

"Go ahead. Come after us. In this storm you'll be lucky if you can find your hand in front of your face."

"Then leave the kid and Doc here," Fargo proposed. "I'll go with you and bring Matt back here to the doctor."

"No. I don't trust you. And that would take too long. Besides, you heard what the doc just said. No. You and the doc are comin' with me, or I take the boy."

Wilder looked at Fargo. Fargo took a deep breath and nodded. Both men knew Melody Clemm would do as she promised. And that meant they had no choice.

Looking back at Melody, Wilder said, "All right. Leave the kid here. I'll go with you. But Fargo doesn't need to come."

"Oh, yes, he does," said Melody. "I ain't goin' to leave him here so he can go on spreadin' lies about us, makin' it impossible for us to stay put."

"Forget it," Fargo told Wilder. He looked then

at Melody. "How we going to get to your wagons in this blizzard?"

"We'll ride. I brought horses. It ain't goin' to be easy in this blizzard. Once we get into the mountains above this town, you two will have to dismount and make paths for the horses."

She hauled the widow Shellabarger's son back into the closet and slammed the door on him, then opened the door to her room and waved them out ahead of her. The moment they stepped out into the night, Fargo and Wilder were almost knocked over by the icy blast that hit them. The three waiting horses were stamping miserably, trying to keep warm.

As they mounted the horses, Melody swung up onto the horse behind them, her revolver still trained on them. Their heads bowed into the wind, they rode out from the rear of the rooming house and almost missed the wooden plank bridge in the swirling snow. They managed to get past it without misadventure, and it was not very long before the snow had closed off all sign of the town behind them.

Once they were above the town, Fargo and Wilder were forced to get off their mounts and break a path for the horses. Melody, wrapped in blankets, stayed mounted. Even through the swirling snow, the two men could catch the glint of her gun barrel.

"It is difficult to believe," panted Wilder as they struggled through one particularly deep drift.

"What is?"

"How a woman so beautiful could be so evil."

Fargo didn't know how to respond to such a comment. Without replying, he pushed on through the drifting snow.

A moment later Wilder spoke up again. "I guess it's the fact that she—and her people—are so completely evil that makes it easy for her. They have no doubts, no feelings of guilt, nothing to restrain them, nothing to make them hold back in the slightest."

Fargo glanced at the struggling, red-faced physician. He was so intent on diagnosing Melody's illness, he hadn't noticed the snow that had built up on his eyebrows or the icicles depending from his chin. Fargo wanted to tell the man to shut up and save his energy for the task ahead of him. Instead, he bent further into the swirling drifts and said nothing.

"Don't you see, Fargo?" Wilder panted. "This is part of her attraction—that she is so completely evil. Have you ever slept with her?"

"Done more than that."

"My God, man, how I envy you," the doctor said, his eyes lit with unashamed lust, "to know intimately a creature of such evil."

"Doc, right now you better save your energy and keep plodding through this snow. You're out of that book-filled room of yours, don't forget. This here is the real world. Look closer at it and forget them fancy ideas. That girl behind us is trouble aplenty. You get sucked into her arms, you ain't likely to come out again—not a whole man, anyway."

Wilder glanced back at Melody. Wrapped in her buffalo robe, she was barely visible as the snow drove past her face. "Yes, yes. Of course," he said. "But she *is* beautiful!"

Fargo looked at the man thoughtfully. He knew Wilder was completely smitten by Melody Clemm. And he understood, despite his apparent impatience with the man.

Fargo had known many women far prettier than Melody Clemm. Indeed, Melody was not very beautiful at all. There was a heaviness about her face at times, and her eyes were perhaps too close together. Yet few women had Melody Clemm's astounding ability to quicken a man. The attraction was in her manner, the promise in her sultry eyes, the vulnerable pout to her lower lip, the feline way she moved, the copious luxuriance of her long hair—above all, it was the incandescent lust she projected. Once enclosed in her arms, a man lost all sense of reality and was drawn into the melting heat of her embrace like a moth into the yawning mouth of hell.

Fargo knew. He had felt that pull more than once.

The wind and snow were finally slacking off when they pulled up in front of the Clemms' wagon. The Clemms had pulled up under a projecting shelf of rock where, about fifty yards away, the ground dropped away into a canyon.

The snow had piled into high drifts all around the wagons, giving the encampment the look of a child's snow fort. A fire was burning behind the wagons. As Melody, still waggling her .38, pushed Fargo and Wilder toward the fire, Pa Clemm and Aaron, wrapped in buffalo robes, got quickly to their feet and came toward them.

Both men were astounded to see Fargo alive. Ma Clemm, peering out of the wagon, let out a shriek of surprise.

"My lan', looks who's here," she cried, stepping eagerly down from the wagon and struggling through the snow toward them.

"You got more lives than a cat, Fargo," announced Pa Clemm.

Aaron looked at Melody. "How'd you find him?"

"The doc told me he was in the town."

"How'd you know enough to ask?"

"I recognized the lies Fargo's been spreadin' about us. Figured he'd be nearby."

"Lies, my ass," said Fargo.

Aaron strode forward casually and with the barrel of his six-gun clubbed Fargo to the ground. Sneering down at Fargo, he said, "The way you tell it, them *is* lies. We never killed anyone wasn't a drifter, a no-account. Not when we was in Kansas, anyhow."

"Where's the wounded man?" Wilder demanded.

"For God sakes, yes," cried Ma Clemm,

110

grabbing Wilder's arm and pulling him toward the wagon. "In here!"

Fargo tried to get up, but Aaron kicked him in the face. "Stay put," he said. He looked at Melody. "Where's the redskin?"

Melody shrugged. "I didn't see him. I thought he'd be with Fargo in his room. But he was gone."

"Then he'll be after us."

"We didn't leave any tracks, not in this storm."

"Don't matter. An Indian can track a bird if he's a mind to."

"So use Fargo as bait," Melody said. "That way we get rid of them both. And we won't have to keep running from the lies these two are spreadin'."

"What about the doc?"

Melody grinned. "He ain't no problem. Just leave him to me."

"Get that rope from the wagon, then. I'll tie this here bastard up good and proper and do like you said—stake him out for bait."

Melody brought a length of Manila rope from one of the wagons and as soon as Aaron began wrapping it around Fargo's wrists, Fargo began kicking out and struggling. Though Aaron beat him about the head and shoulders with the barrel of his six-gun to quiet him, Fargo continued to fight back. He gave Aaron no respite until at last, in order to finish binding him, Aaron was forced to club Fargo unconscious.

*　*　*

Lying awkwardly on his side well away from the fire, Fargo came awake to the sound of Ma Clemm's wailing. Fargo knew at once that Wilder had been unable to save Matt Clemm. Fargo could understand Ma Clemm's grief, even if he could not sympathize. If Aaron was Pa's younger double, Matt was Ma Clemm's. It was difficult to think of this family of monsters capable of emotions as human as grief.

Fargo struggled upright and worked himself over so he could lean back against a boulder. A second later he saw Wilder clambering anxiously down out of the wagon, Ma Clemm following after him, her little fists pounding on his back as he fled before her. Behind Ma Clemm came Melody. She pulled Ma back away from Wilder, then flung her arms around her mother, sobbing.

Free of Ma Clemm, Wilder kept going until he reached Fargo, knelt beside him, and tried to untie him. Aaron ran over and kicked Wilder away from Fargo, then clubbed Wilder on the side of his head with his revolver, knocking him on his ass.

"Aaron!" screamed Melody.

"The son of a bitch was untying Fargo," Aaron replied, straightening up to face his sister.

Not yet unconscious, Wilder reached up and grabbed Aaron. Hauling himself up, he punched Aaron feebly, then tried to grab his weapon out of his hand. Laughing at Wilder's feeble attempt to disarm him, Aaron flung Wilder to the ground and proceeded to kick him about the head and shoulders. Pa Clemm joined his son, and between the two of them, they kicked Wilder with a calm, dogged efficiency until he finally passed out.

Then Pa Clemm dragged Fargo around to the other side of the two wagons and kicked him sprawling into a small clearing within sight of the trail leading from a nearby ridge. Fargo would have frozen to death if Melody hadn't come out and thrown a blanket over him.

She didn't want her plan to use him as a bait for Red Shirt to fail. As she explained angrily to her pa, he'd be no good to them frozen to death.

Red Shirt took out after Fargo and doc the morning after they left. It was easy enough for him to tell what had happened, since Melody's wet boots had left a clear track from the room he shared with Fargo to the back room Melody had taken, and then out to where her horses had waited in the blizzard. All that morning, the fresh horse buns and urine, frozen solid, left a spoor he followed without difficulty into the high white mountains.

Near sundown, Red Shirt poked his head through a snow-laden juniper and peered down at the two wagons. He saw what appeared to be a huddled figure curled up in the snow in front of one of them. At first, he thought it might be a dog. But moving closer, he recognized Fargo's battered face and the snow-encrusted ropes wound about his chest.

Red Shirt did not approach Fargo directly. Pulling back into the snow, he worked his way around to the other side of the wagons. There, about the fire, Ma Clemm and Melody sat on a snow-covered log. Beside Melody, a hot cup of coffee warming his hands, sat Doc Wilder.

Red Shirt waited. After a minute or so, Pa Clemm and Aaron descended from one of the wagons and headed for the fire. When the two men reached it, the smell of fresh coffee came sharply to Red Shirt as Ma Clemm poured out fresh cups of coffee and handed them to Pa and Aaron.

But where was Matt? Red Shirt wondered.

When dusk fell, he crept back to the other side of the wagons, entered one of them, and found Matt's body, his lifeless eyes open and staring up at him from the wagon bed. Satisfied that he had accounted for them all, Red Shirt left the wagon and moved swiftly across the hard-packed snow to Fargo.

He was slicing through the ropes when he heard the snow crunching behind him. Whirling, he saw a gleeful Pa Clemm between the wagons, bringing up his rifle. Beside him Aaron aimed his rifle and fired. Red Shirt flung up his Colt and returned the fire, one of his slugs taking off Pa's wide-brimmed hat. But their slugs tore into Red Shirt's shoulder and side, sending him reeling back into a drift.

He got to his feet, sent another shot back at the two, then ran for cover. A slug caught him in the calf of his right leg, knocking the leg out from under him. The ground opened up beneath him and he went plunging into an abyss. The last thing he remembered, before striking something hard and unyielding, was the dark, snow-clad canyon wall whipping past him. . . .

The firing woke Fargo. Lifting his head, he saw Red Shirt rolling into the snowbank, then come up again miraculously and begin to run, still firing—until he plunged headlong into the canyon.

Fargo turned to see Pa Clemm and Aaron coming toward him. Both men were pleased, their narrow faces split with grins. For a moment, Fargo thought they were going to shoot him in cold blood. Instead, reaching down, they dragged him over to the canyon rim and with a hearty snarl, flung him after the bullet-riddled Red Shirt.

As Fargo felt himself falling, still bound hand and foot, he figured he understood why they had not shot him. A quick, efficient death was not at all what the Clemms wanted for him. With his body broken and torn on the canyon floor, his death would be slow and terrible.

Abruptly, he glanced off a ledge, then felt himself tumbling wildly out of control until he slammed into a snowbank and was momentarily enclosed in wet, smothering darkness. Tumbling on through the snowbank, he was for a brief moment airborne, coming to a sharp, jolting halt against a sapling. He smashed it to the ground beneath him, the heavy rope about his chest absorbing most of the shock.

He blacked out momentarily. When he regained his senses, he thought he could hear the jingle of harnesses high above him as the Clemms pulled out. He thought of Doc Wilder then and wondered what had happened to him—or rather, what Melody had done to him.

It was a black night. Fargo struggled to a sitting position. His struggle while Aaron had been trying to bind him had been for a purpose. With Fargo struggling as hard as he was, Aaron had been unable to do his job efficiently. Now, as a result, Fargo found the rope about his wrists not nearly as tight as it should have been. He noticed that a good deal of the rope around his waist had been sliced through, also. This puzzled him for a moment until he remembered Red Shirt.

After less than a hour, Fargo managed to free his wrists. Then, flinging the rope aside, he stood up and looked around for Red Shirt. He did not expect to find the Indian alive, but he wouldn't leave here before finding out one way or the other. He had started to move on down the canyon when he realized he was in much worse shape than he thought. His left ankle had been sprained or broken. And his right shoulder was numb, but growing steadily more painful.

Then he spotted Red Shirt.

The Indian was lying sprawled facedown in a deep snowdrift. From the look of it, he had not moved since he hit the snow. Under him his blood had melted through the snow, then congealed. As Fargo turned him over, he was almost certain his friend was dead.

But Red Shirt had fooled him. As Fargo bent close, Red Shirt's eyes opened. "Red Shirt is big fool," the Indian growled, his dark, round face showing no emotion. "He let Clemms bushwhack him."

"Never mind that," Fargo told him, hastily examining the Indian's wounds. "You're hurt bad."

"Bullets go through Indian. Leave holes. Maybe I dead soon. You cover me with snow so wolves not get me."

"Like hell," said Fargo, ripping away at his own buckskin shirt to make bandages. "I'm bringing you back to Red Gap."

Red Shirt closed his eyes.

"Leave me, Fargo. Red Gap too far. This is good place to die."

Fargo ignored Red Shirt's words, finished bandaging his three wounds, then slung the Indian over his shoulder. The problem was getting to his feet and staying on them. The shock of his fall had worn off completely by this time, and he could feel now how badly his right shoulder had been pounded. And with every step he took, his left ankle protested and was soon swollen so badly inside his boot, the ankle went numb from lack of circulation. Switching Red

Shirt's body from first one shoulder to the other, Fargo kept pushing himself on down the canyon.

Through the night Fargo staggered, stopping constantly to rest and pull himself together. By midmorning, gasping painfully in the thin atmosphere, he collapsed into a snowbank, Red Shirt still draped over his back. A couple of miles below him was Red Gap. The town was a distant series of snow-covered roofs, wood smoke coiling up from them. By this time Fargo knew that he couldn't possibly carry Red Shirt down those sheer, snow-covered slopes to the valley below.

Red Shirt stirred. His eyes opened.

"I'm going to leave you here," Fargo told Red Shirt. "But I'll be back for you."

"Sure."

"If I can't make it myself, I'll send someone back for you."

Red Shirt closed his eyes.

Taking off his buckskin jacket, Fargo wrapped it around Red Shirt, then started for the valley below. At times he sank into the drifts and let himself be carried on down the slope, falling ever lower, sometimes gently, sometimes with brutal, numbing speed. A couple of times he came up hard against his right shoulder, but he gritted his teeth and kept on. At last, dazed and battered, he came to rest on the valley floor in a drift so deep that for a while he despaired of being able to burrow his way out.

Free of the drift, he headed for the town. The

plank bridge was in sight when finally he gave out, collapsing to the ground. What aroused him was the sound of a townsman driving a sleigh past him. The townsman passed Fargo without looking to the right or left. Fargo tried to call out to him, but the sleigh's bells drowned out his feeble cries. To add to his frustration, a horseman dragging a platform for firewood rode past him without catching sight of him even though Fargo waved frantically.

Disgusted, Fargo pushed himself erect and staggered across the plank bridge, keeping on until he reached the saloon. He managed to climb to the saloon porch before collapsing a second time. Only dimly was he aware of excited voices above him and of hands pulling him over onto his back.

When he opened his eyes, the brilliant blue sky burned into them and he flinched away. There was a concerted gasp as those above him saw his condition. He was carried into the saloon and put down on two tables dragged together.

Barely conscious, he grabbed the shirt of an old-timer leaning close. "Up there on the cliff . . . Red Shirt . . . wounded. Get him down!"

"Red Shirt? That your buddy?"

Fargo nodded weakly. "He'll die up there. . . ."

The old-timer glanced at someone standing beside him. The fellow shrugged, as if to say, why not?

"Okay, mister," said the old-timer, looking back at Fargo. "We'll get your Indian."

Fargo told him where he'd left Red Shirt.

"We won't have no trouble getting him down," the old-timer promised. "Rest easy now."

The hum of voices around Fargo faded quickly. The last thing he remembered was the relief he felt when a gentle hand worked the boot off his swollen left foot.

8

How long he had been out of it Fargo had no idea. He awoke famished. The sun glancing off the snow filled his room with a diffused light so soft, even celestial, he thought for a crazy moment he might have died and gone to heaven.

The moment he turned his head, he knew he was in one of the rooms beyond Doc Wilder's office. His powerful body made the cot he was resting on sag almost to the floor. Flinging back the blankets covering, he sat up.

This sudden movement startled the woman sitting in a chair in the corner, a half-knitted wool sweater in her lap. Immediately she put the sweater aside and hurried over to him. He saw it was the widow Shellabarger.

"Good afternoon, Mr. Fargo," she said, smiling. "How do you feel?"

"Hungry."

"I shouldn't wonder."

"How long have I been up here?"

"This will be your fourth day."

"What time is it?"

"About two."

"Then I missed the noon meal, huh?"

It was an attempt to make her smile and succeeded. "I am sure something can be arranged, Mr. Fargo."

"Call me, Fargo."

"And you may call me Helen."

Fargo looked anxiously about him. "Where's Red Shirt, Helen? Did they find him?"

"Yes, they found him. He's in the next room, asleep. It will take a while longer for him to recover fully, I am afraid. He lost a great deal of blood."

"But he'll be all right?"

She nodded, smiling again. "Like you, Fargo, he is a very tough man to kill, it seems." Then she became serious. "What about Doctor Wilder? Didn't he go off with you?"

"I guess he's still with the Clemms, the poor son of a bitch."

"They took him with them? Why?"

Fargo shrugged. "I think Melody had something to do with it."

Helen seemed to sag.

Fargo looked more closely at her. "Were you and the doc close friends?"

"It was . . . more than that. But I suppose he was attracted by that woman's . . . boldness." Helen shook her head as she recalled Melody standing in her door asking for a room for the

122

night. "I can still see her, Fargo. There was a look about her, as if there were nothing she would not do to satisfy her lusts or those of any man." Helen shrugged wearily. "If Doctor Wilder has joined with such a woman, I can't blame him. I don't believe there's a man in this world able to refuse her."

Fargo said nothing. Helen was right. After all, he had certainly not refused Melody, and he had no doubt that by now Wilder had proven no less vulnerable."

"I think I'd like to get up and move around," he said. "Give me some help, will you?"

Taking his hand, Helen pulled him gently up off the cot. Fargo stood in place for a moment, balancing himself precariously as the floor seemed to tip beneath him; then he let Helen lead him over to a window. Once there, he found himself looking down at Red Gap's main street. He saw dark, muddy patches on it where the snow had already melted.

"It looks warm out," he said.

"It is. Very warm. That early storm was only a freak."

"Or a warning."

Looking beyond the plank bridge, Fargo saw about twenty wagons parked in a round circle, the settlers who owned them moving about between the canvas-topped wagons like busy ants.

"The town's got visitors, I see."

"They are going to try to make it through the pass to California before winter closes in."

"They might make it."

"Yes."

Feeling suddenly dizzy, Fargo turned gingerly and allowed the widow to help him back to his cot. Once he was safely sitting on it, he thanked her.

As she turned to leave him, he asked, "Helen, how's your boy?"

Her face went cold, the lines in it hardening as she told him about her finding her son in the closet in Melody Clemm's room, still bound securely, the gag wound so tightly about the boy's mouth and nose that he had almost suffocated to death. It would have been a truly terrible way for him to have died.

"Is he all right now?"

"Yes. But I hear him tossing at night. You can imagine what it must be like for him now to wake up in a dark room. The sheer terror . . ."

"I'm sorry," Fargo said lamely.

"I blame myself. I didn't want to give that woman a room. Something told me to turn her away. But the snow was coming down so hard and it was so cold outside, I just couldn't do it."

"How could you have known something like that would happen?"

"That's what everyone tells me. Anyway, it's time I went to get you some nourishment. Would you like some hot soup?"

"How long will it take?"

"It's already cooking."

"Good," he told her. "But hurry or you'll find me outside eating the bark off the trees."

"Well, now," she replied, brightening, "I wouldn't want that."

She hurried from the room.

It was a few days later, around midnight, when Fargo heard the outside door open, followed by the sound of Helen Shellabarger's familiar footsteps approaching him through the doctor's office. He sat up and swung his feet off the cot. Unable to sleep, he had been staring up at the ceiling, listening to a coyote off somewhere in the distance yelping at the full moon.

"What are you doing up?" she asked, pausing beside his cot. "You should be sleeping."

"I could ask you the same thing."

"I'm worried about Red Shirt," she told him, continuing on into the next room. "He didn't finish his supper."

Without moving, he waited for the widow to return. She wouldn't be long, Fargo knew. Red Shirt was doing fine. He'd been prowling around most of the day, peering out through the window with Fargo, like him eager to get after the Clemms.

The townspeople had sort of adopted them once they had been told about the Clemms and the reason why Fargo and Red Shirt were pursuing them. For the last couple of days, there had been visitors aplenty, most of them anxious

125

to hear about the infamous family. That very afternoon, the head of the town council had stopped up to ask how they were doing.

Helen left Red Shirt's room, closing the door softly behind her. On her way out, she paused once again by Fargo's cot.

"You two are very tough men, it seems," she said. "Red Shirt is sleeping like a baby. How do you feel?"

He shrugged and smiled up at her through the darkness. "The ankle feels strong enough now for me to ride, and my shoulder has only a slight twinge in it. Lucky, I guess."

"Yes, you certainly are."

He got up from the cot and walked with Helen to the door leading onto the wooden landing. Opening it for her, they stepped out onto it. The street was silent below them, and the silver-dollar moon hung high over the town, sending its spectral glow over the rooftops, as if a second, lighter snowfall had followed the first.

Pausing with her hand on the railing, Helen turned to Fargo. "Good night," she said.

"Good night, Helen," he replied. "Thanks for stopping up."

She nodded. Then, without moving on down the stairs as she had intended, she turned to look at him. In that instant, he knew what she needed, what she had come up here to find.

"What is it, Helen?" he asked her gently.

For reply, she opened her mouth slightly and pressed her lips to his. He kissed her back. Then, holding her in his arms, he guided her back into the room and led her over to his cot, easing her gently down onto it. She lifted her face to his, and he found himself kissing her just as hungrily as she had been kissing him. Her lips were hot, yet soft, returning his hungry desire with a whole-hearted passion that kindled him instantly. There were no words. None were needed as he pulled her close to him. His hands worked quickly to remove her clothes, with her helping all she could.

Soon their naked bodies were clasped together in a feverish embrace. He was barely aware of entering her, but he felt her gasp, her breath quickening, her tightening convulsively about him as he began slowly, ever so slowly, to thrust. Deeper and deeper he went, her long legs closing about him as she met him thrust for thrust. It was a fierce, silent coupling, their two bodies cleaving to each other, becoming one. Only gradually did the tempo increase. Her arms tightened about his neck and he pulled her still closer, pressing deep, deep into her as they rocked on the edge of fulfillment. And then, surprisingly, with no panting or thrashing, he slipped over the edge.

She cried out softly as she felt him emptying into her, and began to shudder from head to toe, a tiny gasp of pleasure breaking from her lips. Then, still clinging to him, a long, deep sigh escaped her. Reluctantly, she loosened her arms from about his neck, her face buried in his shoulder, her body still warm against his. For the first time Fargo realized what it meant to ease a woman.

He eased out of her and began stroking her hair. She murmured softly and moved still closer to him. After a while she said something about her hoping he would understand her need for him.

"You sorry it happened?" he asked her gently, still stroking her head.

"Oh, no, Fargo."

"Then don't say anything else."

She sighed, worked herself still closer to him, and was soon fast asleep in his arms.

Smiling, Fargo got himself as comfortable as he could on the narrow cot, closed his eyes, and fell into a deep, dreamless sleep.

Three nights later Fargo and Helen were sitting on the landing in front of Doc Wilder's office, Fargo puffing on a cigar, Helen still knitting the wool sweater, guiding her swift needles by the moon's pale light. Red Shirt was asleep inside after having spent the day hiking about the town, even visiting the settlers as they made ready to pull out. A few hours before, a slight grin on his face, he had assured Fargo that his presence had alarmed more than a few of the nervous pilgrims.

"Fargo," Helen said abruptly, "I've sold the rooming house."

Fargo took the cigar out of his mouth. "Who'd you sell it to?"

"One of the settlers. It was more a swap than a

sale. My rooming house for his wagon and stock. He even threw in a piano with the rest of his furniture. His name is Norton. He came all the way from Philadelphia, and his family is pretty weary by now. I just want to get away, Fargo. To California. Oregon. Anywhere."

"You think you'll be able to handle that wagon with just you and the boy?"

"I heard you and Red Shirt talking. I know you're going after the Clemms."

Fargo simply nodded.

"And you're leaving tomorrow, joining up with the wagon train."

"I was going to tell you later. The wagon master was glad to have us along to help him scout. He's not sure of this country, and there's always a chance of more snow before they get across the divide."

"Then travel in my wagon—you and Red Shirt."

"We're just going with the wagon train because it's going the same way the Clemms were heading. There's no telling how long we'll stay with it."

"I know that. But I don't care. This town is no place to bring up a boy. I want schools for him, a chance to make something of himself. This town is going nowhere, Fargo."

Fargo considered Helen's offer as he put his cigar back into his mouth. He could understand her desire to get out of this backwater. Further, Fargo had figured out that, before he came, she had been hoping Doc Wilder would take her from the place. But he was gone now—and the way she saw it, Fargo was her last hope.

"Okay, Helen. We'll go in your wagon. Thanks. That'll sure make it easier for us."

"For me, too, Fargo."

"Of course, like I just said, I can't promise that Red Shirt and I'll be going all the way to California. If we're lucky, we'll catch up with the Clemms and take after them."

"I understand, Fargo."

Fargo stuck his cigar back into his mouth and Helen went back to her knitting, the needles moving at a less hectic pace now, their faint click lulling Fargo. A few minutes later he flung his cigar's glowing butt into the darkness and went inside. Not long after, Helen followed in after him.

A week later Fargo and Red Shirt were moving through a thick stand of timber, hunting for fresh game. That morning Helen and her boy had admitted they were getting pretty sick of salt pork, and the two men felt the same way.

It wasn't snowing. Instead, it was raining— steadily, drearily. They had picketed their horses and for the past five minutes had been moving on foot through the drenched woodland. When at last they stopped on the edge of a mist-covered clearing, Fargo found himself thinking longingly of the dry Conestoga wagon he and Red Shirt had left behind.

"Don't move," said Red Shirt, peering intently across the clearing.

But Fargo had not needed the warning. A large buck had appeared like an apparition out of the light, shifting curtains of rain obscuring the meadowland. It was a ten-pointer, at least, larger than a mule deer, with glowing, yellowish red on its breast and belly.

As silent and as immobile as statues, both men watched the buck's stately approach, its antlered head moving quickly from side to side as it tested the air for sign of possible predators. Still well out of rifle range, the buck halted and looked back at the edge of the clearing from which it had emerged. At once a doe and a yearling stepped out of the timber after it, then moved swiftly into the meadow and proceeded to browse.

Then it was the buck's turn to feed. The moment its head bent to the grass, both men stepped closer, moving stealthily forward until a whisk of the buck's black tail alerted them. They froze as the deer's head shot up. It looked directly at them through the rain for a long moment, then swung its gaze to their right, sweeping the entire clearing with its imperious glance. It had seen them, but since neither man had moved a muscle, the buck regarded them as nothing more dangerous than a tree or a stand of brush.

The buck resumed its browsing. Farther back, pale shadows in the mistlike rainfall, the doe and its yearling continued to crop the grass as well. Fargo and Red Shirt edged closer to the buck, being careful to move in such a way that they could halt instantly if need be. Twice more the buck was alerted. Each time it gazed carefully at the two frozen hunters for a moment or so, then looked swiftly about and dropped its head to resume its feeding.

Within range at last, Fargo carefully brought up his rifle, aimed, and fired. To his dismay, he managed only to powder one of the buck's antlers. In an instant, the buck, the doe, and the yearling were in full flight. Beside Fargo Red Shirt fired at the fleeing buck and and brought it down.

"Nice shooting, Red Shirt," Fargo said. "Guess I was a little too anxious."

The Indian shrugged without comment, only his gleaming black eyes showing the pleasure he felt at having bested a white man in such a contest. Without further discussion, the two men hastened into the clearing to procure the fresh venison they had just harvested.

A good three hours later, as the two men overtook the wagon train, the rain had turned to snow and the wind had picked up considerably. Helen and the boy were glad to see them as they tied their horses to the rear of the wagon and hefted the dead buck into it. Red Shirt had used his knife to skin the animal. The butchering would take the rest of the night. But that didn't matter. It was fresh meat, and it looked like a long spell of bad weather was descending on them.

"We're in for a long blow," Fargo said to Helen as he got warm standing next to her. The boy was up front, driving the horses.

"Now you see why I wanted you to come with us?"

"That the only reason?"

She just looked at him and smiled.

But she was not smiling an hour or so later as the wagon train moved up a long steep grade through a snow squall so fierce that at times Fargo, who had taken the reins from her boy by this time, had difficulty seeing the wagon just ahead of them.

Toward nightfall the wagon master, Kimberly Masters, rode back along the wagon train and swung into the wagon to find a seat beside Fargo. "We're going to have to stop here," he shouted above the roar of the wind.

"No," Fargo shouted back. "If we get caught on this slope tonight, we'll never get off it. We've got to keep going until we find protection from the wind."

"We *can't* go on," Masters told him. "It'll be dark soon and already the lead wagon's driver says he can't see ten feet ahead of him. And the rest of the drivers can barely see the wagon in front of them."

"Tell the lead wagon to keep going. Tell him we'll follow his tracks in the snow. It's the only way, even if we have to leave the wagons and lead our horses."

"Not that driver. He's scared, Fargo. He might lead us all off a cliff!"

"All right. I'll take the lead wagon," Fargo said.

Masters swung out of the wagon and rode back to the lead wagon as Fargo untied his pinto from the rear of the wagon and rode on ahead through the driving snow. When he reached the lead wagon, he tied his pinto to the rear of it, then clambered up into the wagon and joined the driver, named Hunter. The man handed Fargo the reins and moved back to join his family, peering grudgingly at Fargo as the Trailsman settled himself on his seat.

Night fell and the snow grew deeper, whipping into drifts with frightening speed. The horses ducked their heads low and kept pulling, but at a slower and slower pace. Fargo shivered under his slicker as it became heavy with the accumulation of snow and was forced to squint continuously in order to see through the sleet-laden wind that lashed at his face and eyes.

At last, as the darkness became almost stygian, from just outside the wagon came Hunter's frantic cry: "We can't go on, Mr. Fargo! We must stop to make camp. It's too dark! The wagons will get lost!"

Fargo poked his head out of the wagon. Hunter was a white apparition, his body and horse covered almost entirely with snow. "Shut up!" Fargo told him. "And get me a bottle of bourbon!"

To Fargo's surprise Hunter turned his horse and beat back through the howling wind, only to return not long after with a bottle of bourbon held in his gloved hand.

Fargo nodded his thanks, took the bourbon, and unstoppered it. Tipping the bottle, he drank deep and drove on through the howling night, the liquor warming his insides clear down to his bootstraps. By this time his cheekbones and nose stung with a touch of frostbite, and his hands, despite his buckskin gloves, were getting numb—so numb, in fact, that on one occasion he almost dropped the bourbon.

They were still climbing. Every once in a while, the swirling curtains of snow would part long enough for him to see the great shouldering side of the mountain that loomed on their right. They were rising steadily toward the pass and had to keep going or they'd never make it. Caught on this exposed ridge, they'd soon be buried alive, wagons and all. For the rest of fall and on through winter, he knew, the snowfall at this altitude would be nearly constant, the depth reaching as much as thirty or more feet before the spring thaws commenced.

They had no choice. They *had* to keep going.

"Hunter!" Fargo barked. "Look out through the back! Are the wagons still behind us?"

A moment later Hunter reported to Fargo that he was able to glimpse at least two wagons through the driving snow. He couldn't see beyond that. Fargo was satisfied. It was better than he had expected. As long as the wagons kept up and managed to stay in his tracks, they wouldn't get lost. But if any of them lagged too far behind, the wind would obliterate the tracks of the wagon in front of them and the wagon train would disintegrate as each wagon went blundering off into the night, lost in a howling, white hell.

Suddenly Fargo could feel the ground beneath the wagon level off. They had reached the pass! A half-hour later, the trail began to drop, giving heart to the horses as they lifted their heads and steadily increased their pace. At the same time Fargo noticed a less shrill cry to the wind, now that he was no longer close under the mountain wall that had been funneling it past him. The snow was no less blinding and no less cold, yet somehow it had lost some of its menace. Soon, Fargo hoped, they would reach the treeline, leaving the worst of the storm behind them.

But it took longer than Fargo had hoped, and for at least three more hours, he drove his exhausted, stumbling team on. By this time, the wind and driving snow had shifted to his back, and the wind no longer howled with such demented consistency. He began glimpsing rifts in the clouds and through them caught sight of stars winking high overhead.

He reached the timber finally, just as the snow-fall and the wind slackened off. Visibility improved markedly and a clear moon sailed into view overhead, casting a sheen over the snow-covered wilderness about him. Catching sight of a wooded benchland under a sheltering ridge, Fargo turned off the trail toward it. A few minutes later they were in a meadowland sheltered by towering pines. His frozen bones creaking, Fargo climbed down from Hunter's wagon to watch the trail behind him for the rest of the wagons.

First came one wagon, then a second, materializing out of the snow's shifting gloom like ships in a fog. There was a long interval before the third wagon hove into view, but after that they came in a steady stream.

Leaving Hunter with his wagon, Fargo untied his pinto and rode back through the deep snow to Helen's wagon. She was still up on the seat with her boy, her mittened hands still clutching the reins.

Fargo was proud of them both.

The settlers made camp hoping that the storm had broken and that they would soon be on their way after a day's rest. The storm had other ideas. It continued to swirl over them, breaking off for hours at a time, only to arouse itself for another fierce, blinding attempt to bury them. At times it seemed as if some angry giant were emptying out his pillow over their heads.

Still, the pines took most of the storm's brunt, and the settlers, aware that they were now safely over the pass, turned their circle of wagons into a kind of snow city, with tracks beaten into the drifts from one wagon to another, and igloolike huts popping up everywhere, the handiwork of the wagon train's young people determined to make the most of this wondrous heavy snowfall.

But hunger soon reared its head, and the pleasant little snow city high in the mountains quieted down. As usual, the settlers had not brought enough with them to handle this long a time on the trail. Their tins of food were nearly gone, and they had no jerky. What fresh vegetables they had brought with them were either rotten or consumed. And the buck Fargo and Red Shirt had brought in before the storm would not last much longer in feeding the entire group.

So Fargo and Red Shirt organized a few settlers into a hunting party and led them into the snowy wilderness in search of fresh game. For two days they ranged the white wilderness, with only the track of one bear—a grizzly by the size of him—to give them any hope.

On the third day Red Shirt told Fargo it would be better if just the two of them went in search of game. Fargo agreed. The other men had quarreled constantly and it was clear from the way they handled their rifles that they would have been more of an obstacle than help if any game had been sighted.

"I got plan," said Red Shirt as soon as they had left the wagons behind.

"I'm listening."

"Grizzly bears. They fat now just before they sleep."

"How we going to find them? Dig them out?"

"Yes."

Fargo pulled up and grinned at the Indian. "Now, wait a minute."

"I not make joke. Before this, I find grizzly den. But I not tell you. Now I have plan."

"You really mean we're going to dig a grizzly out of his den?"

"No. Not you. Me. For Red Shirt, grizzly is good medicine."

At once Fargo understood. During rites that induced hallucinations, some Indians had visions of a particular animal—a fox or an eagle or a coyote—and from then on, that animal would become the Indian's invisible protector, the animal to whom the Indian would pray before battle. When Red Shirt's vision had come, it seemed, he had seen a grizzly.

"How do you plan on doing this, Red Shirt? You going to walk in there and poke him with your rifle and tell him he's needed someplace else."

"I will poke grizzly. Then I will run. You will shoot grizzly when he chase me out."

"Suppose you don't *get* out?"

Red Shirt shook his head emphatically. "Grizzly no kill me."

"You sure of that, are you?"

Red Shirt looked at Fargo. "We talk too much. Come."

With a shrug, Fargo followed Red Shirt into the pines and started climbing through the timber, heading for a long white slope that gleamed at them through the trees.

Not until Red Shirt had poked a long slender sapling in under the bank and Fargo had seen how far in it went did he believe that Red Shirt had indeed found a grizzly's den. Red Shirt straightened up and cast aside the sapling. Then he took out his long skinning knife and turned to Fargo.

"You sure gun is loaded, powder dry?"

"This Sharp is as ready as it ever will be," Fargo assured his friend. "I just wish to hell you'd think of some other way to get that bear out."

"No. We get it this way. I have dream."

Fargo looked around, saw a downed tree about ten yards back. He moved behind it and sighted on the den's entrance. He had a clear shot, the downed tree would steady his aim, and he had never missed at this range. Still, his mouth was getting dry and his hands sweaty as he gripped the rifle stock and crouched down into the snow piled behind the tree trunk.

"I go in now," said Red Shirt."

Fargo said nothing as Red Shirt went down on his hands and knees and moved in under the bank to disappear a moment later into the grizzly's den. Crazy Indian, Fargo thought unhappily as he rested his finger gently on the Sharps' trigger and sighted along the barrel.

And prayed.

9

When Red Shirt reappeared, he was not running. He emerged from under the embankment, stood up and shook himself. He seemed more than a little discouraged as he squinted at Fargo through the sunlight slanting up off the snow-covered slope.

Fargo relaxed and smiled in relief. There was evidently no grizzly in this particular den. Better luck next time, he told himself, pushing forward the Sharp's safety catch.

Then, abruptly, for some damn-fool reason, Red Shirt started to run toward Fargo.

"Behind you, Fargo," Red Shirt cried.

Fargo spun. The big grizzly he had expected to come charging out after Red Shirt was shambling toward Fargo instead, and was less than ten feet away his jaw open, his red tongue lolling. The huge male bear was moving at an incredibly fast, rolling gait, his hump rising and falling, his mad eyes locked on Fargo's.

Releasing the catch in one swift movement, Fargo brought up his Sharps and sent a round at the ridge between the grizzly's eyes. The bullet slammed into the bear's snout, demolishing it. Even with a slug in his brain, however, the grizzly did not slow. Fargo flung himself to one side. The great, shambling beast charged past, swiping at him as it did so. Fargo felt the needle-sharp claws flick across his ass as he landed in the snow on the other side of the tree trunk.

Rolling over, Fargo found himself looking up at the wounded beast. His shattered face was dripping, the claws on his forepaws extended as he measured Fargo for one quick, final swipe. Fargo still had his Sharps, but no time to reload it. He flung it at the bear, catching him on the side of his head. The rifle glanced off, the infuriated animal barely noticing it.

The grizzly reared up on all fours. Fargo drew his six-gun and pumped one, two, three rounds into the massive chest. The bullets rocked the grizzly back slightly, a wild red light leaping into his tiny eyes. Reaching down with one paw, he flung the fallen tree trunk aside as easily as if it were a twig. Fargo fired twice, but his position was so awkward both bullets sang past the bear's head. Then his hammer came down on an empty chamber.

Red Shirt appeared behind the grizzly. One leap and he was riding the bear's back, his arm wrapped securely around the animal's powerful neck. The grizzly staggered back and went down on all fours, shifting with fury as he tried to dislodge Red Shirt. But the Indian could not be shaken loose as he plunged his long knife over and over into the grizzly's chest, finishing him off at last with a single upward slash that severed the animal's jugular.

The huge bear staggered drunkenly, a gout of dark blood pouring from his neck. Red Shirt jumped clear. Doggedly, the bear tried to catch him with one final swipe of his paw. Red Shirt danced nimbly aside and the grizzly slumped over, steam coming from the snow as his hot blood sank through it.

Fargo got to his feet and felt his ass. His buckskin britches were sticky with blood. But he would live. "Thanks, Red Shirt."

Red Shirt shrugged. "This bear not belong to this den. We just lucky, looks like."

"You call that luck?"

"Sure. You alive. Me alive. And we have much meat for settlers. You go get horses, I make travois," he said.

"You think we'll need both horses?"

"What you think?" asked Red Shirt, glancing down at the great, sprawled beast.

The grizzly was as big a grizzly as Fargo had ever seen. Eight feet tall if it was an inch. And fat, its body rolling in suet after a summer of berries and other goodies in preparation for his long winter's nap.

Fargo glanced back at Red Shirt and nodded. "Reckon we'll need both horses."

As Red Shirt started toward a nearby slope, Fargo hurried off to get the horses. When he returned, he saw Red Shirt still on the slope, slashing through saplings for the travois. Leaving the horses beside the dead bear, Fargo waded up the slope through the heavy snowdrifts and was within about twenty yards of Red Shirt when he saw another bear come shambling down the slope behind the Indian.

"Watch out, Red Shirt!" Fargo cried. "Another bear!"

As Fargo raised his rifle to cut down the bear, Red Shirt whirled just in time to catch the bear's charge. The two went down behind a snowdrift, both struggling fiercely. Unwilling to fire for fear of hitting Red Shirt, Fargo pulled himself desperately through the snow and was close enough to fire on the bear when Red Shirt flung him aside and staggered erect.

"Hell, Fargo! This no bear!"

Fargo pushed closer and found himself looking down at the ravaged face of Doc Wilder.

While the settlers' butcher set to work on the huge grizzly, a circle of happy settlers crowding him, Helen was in her wagon bent over Doc Wilder. With a warm cloth she was laving his frostbitten face. Though he was conscious, Wilder had been unable to give any of them a coherent account of his sudden appearance on that steep pine slope.

"Help me get his clothes off," Helen told Fargo and Red Shirt.

When they had done so, they were shocked at Wilder's appearance. His frame was skeletal, and about his ankles were huge, festering sores and on his back, broadly, ugly welts where he had been whipped.

At once Helen wrapped him warmly in sheets and a blanket and vanished out the rear of the wagon to see to the venison stew her boy was helping her to prepare.

As soon as she was gone, Fargo leaned close to the doctor. "Wilder!" he said. "Can you hear me?"

Wilder's head turned slightly. He opened his eyes and stared up at Fargo for a moment, obviously straining to see him clearly in the single lantern's dim light.

"It's Fargo," Fargo said, prompting him.

Recognition flooded Wilder's eyes. Then they narrowed in a kind of mad fear. "You mean I'm not back in the Clemm's wagon?"

"I sure as hell hope not."

He looked past Fargo at Red Shirt and smiled feebly. "And you aren't any bear, are you?"

Red Shirt allowed himself a soft chuckle.

Helen returned with the venison stew and shooed them both out. It was clear now that, once she had Doc Wilder back, she was not going to let him out of her sight.

Around a crackling campfire a day later, Doc

Wilder, wrapped warmly in a blanket Helen had thrown over him, was busy telling the two men of his escape from the Clemms.

". . . so, as soon as they thought they had killed you two," Wilder said, glancing at Fargo and Red Shirt, "they lashed their horses and headed for this pass. Aaron had me tied up good and proper, but Melody saw to it that I was free to eat and move around whenever it was necessary for me to do so."

"She was a real comfort to you, then."

Wilder glanced over toward Helen's wagon, where the woman was busy inside repairing his garments, her boy asleep beside her. Certain she was not within hearing distance, Wilder looked back at Fargo. "Yes. You are right. Melody did all she could to comfort me—and herself," Wilder admitted wearily. "Never in all my life has a woman used me so voraciously. But I tell you in all honesty, gentlemen, it is not something I would ever want to experience again."

"You mean you didn't like it?" Fargo prompted, taking the cigar from his mouth and smiling across the fire at Wilder.

"Let's put it this way. Sometimes when a man gets what he thinks he wants, he finds he really doesn't want it all that bad."

"Too much of a good thing, that it?"

"Precisely."

"Go on, Wilder."

"I tried to escape them twice. The second time Aaron insisted on keeping me tied up all the time.

By that time we had joined up with other settlers heading for the pass."

"How many wagons were there?"

"Three."

"Go on."

"The trouble was, the fellow leading the other three wagons thought he knew a quicker route over the mountains. He didn't. And when the next storm hit, we were trapped in a narrow valley high above the pass."

"You mean they're still up there? The Clemms?"

"Yes. Starving to death." He shuddered. "I was able to escape because my wrists had shrunk so, the rope just slipped off."

Fargo thought that over. The Clemms were trapped on some peak high above him at that very moment, snowed in completely, waiting for the white death of starvation. Yet, he found that hard to believe. The Clemms were too tough to go that quietly.

Fargo looked at Wilder. "You think you could show me how to get up there."

"Leave them, Fargo. They're done for."

"I can't be sure of that. And I sure don't like to think of them surviving somehow, then setting up a boardinghouse in California or anywhere else."

Wilder took a deep breath and shook his head. "I admit that's not a pleasant thought."

Moving off the log he was sitting on, Wilder drew a rough map in the snow, indicating the mountain peak Fargo should aim for to reach the narrow valley where the Clemms and their companions were trapped.

"Was it snowing when you left?" Fargo asked.

"It snows all the time up there, Fargo. Sometimes, around noon, it lets up. But I wouldn't count on it."

"Sounds like hell, sure enough," commented Fargo.

Helen stepped down out of the wagon, Wilder's pants and vest folded across her arm. Stopping beside the fire, she handed them to Wilder. Wilder thanked her as he took them from her.

"I'll work on your coat tomorrow," she told him, smiling warmly. "Jim Hunter says he has a hat you can have."

"Tell Jim thanks," Wilder said, returning to the wagon to try on his repaired britches.

As soon as Wilder had vanished into the wagon, Helen turned to glance at Fargo and Red Shirt. "I guess you've heard about the Clemms. Are you going after them?"

"Tomorrow," Fargo admitted.

"I almost wish I could go with you. The thought of that family and that woman still alive makes me shudder."

"It don't make us feel any too good, either."

"I wish you luck. Be careful."

Fargo was thinking of Helen's warning when—a week later—he and Red Shirt reached the wagons. Their climb up to this height had been a two-day ordeal through a frigid hell as they pulled themselves up through deep drifts and across patches of ice capable of causing either man to plunge off the mountain to his death. Now, peering through a swirling curtain of snow, they saw the five wagons below them, locked solidly in a massive snowdrift.

Fargo caught some movement near the wagons. An old man was moving along a well-beaten path; he appeared to be limping slightly.

"Someone's down there, all right," Fargo remarked.

Red Shirt glanced sidelong at him, his black eyes gleaming. "It will be dark soon. We go in then?"

"Better plan this out. I say we make camp for the night and get under cover. I'm freezing."

They pushed themselves off the ridge and worked their way back down the steep slope to a spot where they could put up the small tent a member of the wagon train had lent them. Soon, under a sheltering rock face, wrapped in blankets, they were fairly impregnable to the razor-sharp winds that began howling about them as soon as the sun dipped below the horizon.

When they awoke the next morning, they found their flimsy tent had collapsed under the weight of the new snow that had fallen overnight. What had awakened them was a corner of the tent flapping furiously in the fierce wind and snow.

About noon, the snow let up and the clouds hovering so close overhead broke up and hurried on to the east. Anxious to get on with their mission, the two men hastened back up the slope, reaching the ridge just as a bright sky and a hot sun appeared overhead.

Fargo pointed to the lead wagon. "You start from there. I'll take this wagon beneath me. I figure all we got to do is work our way toward each other."

"We take prisoners?"

"If they let us."

Red Shirt patted his knife, then spun the cylinders of his Colt, dropped it into his holster, and slipped down through the snow. Fargo also checked his Colt, waited to give Red Shirt enough time to reach the distant wagon, then worked his way down through the drifts, anxious not to betray his presence by starting a small avalanche.

When he reached the wagons, he was startled to find them empty, stripped clean. What he had seen from above were only the canvas tops, which had been left in place as a sort of rough shelter from the wind and snow. The rest of the wagons—their sides and flooring—had been broken up and carted away. Moving down the line of wagons along the path he had noticed from above, he saw that it led to a tunnel cut into the massive snowdrift.

But where was everybody? There was no traffic at all among the wagons. No sign of life. The entire encampment was spectrally quiet. Fargo looked around for Red Shirt, but the Indian seemed to have vanished as well. Deciding not to wait for him, Fargo ducked into the tunnel.

Almost at once Fargo heard voices ahead of him and ducked to one side, leaning into the hard-packed snow. But the voices did not get closer and gradually faded. Fargo started up again, turned a corner, and saw just ahead of him a crude wooden door in the snowbank that had been constructed from boards taken from the wagons.

Fargo pushed open the door and stepped inside. He found himself in a long room containing a series of bunks separated by wooden panels. The cold was intense. Wooden planks had been laid down through the center of the room. There was a door at the far end. Fargo moved swiftly along the planks, listened for a moment at the door, then pushed it open. A smoking oil lamp sat on an empty crate in the center of the room.

"Well, now," came a voice from beside Fargo. "I thought I heard someone. Turn around, mister, and tell me where the hell you dropped from."

Fargo spun to see a lean, cadaverous settler in a floppy hat and baggy overalls. He looked as old as Methuselah and was leaning on a makeshift crutch. One empty pants leg was folded up neatly, a huge safety pin holding it in place. In his right hand he held a shotgun, the twin bores staring up at Fargo.

"Just dropped in," Fargo told him easily. "Surprised?"

"I sure as hell am. The only thing movin' up here's eagles or the damn wind. Step lively now. It's too cold in here."

With the stranger poking him in the rear with his shotgun, Fargo continued on through the small passage into a large, windowless room. The first thing he noticed was the warmth of a wood fire. The walls were lined with more boards ripped from the wagons, and the room was filled with an odd assortment of furniture taken from the wagons. Two doorways led off to other rooms, probably bedrooms.

A very old woman was making coffee at a wood stove in the corner. A halo of white hair hung about her head, and she was wearing at least three heavy woolen sweaters. Trussed up like turkeys in the far corner were Pa and Aaron Clemm. They stared in amazement as Fargo entered.

"Dammit all to hell," said Pa Clemm, shaking his head in wonder. "I thought I killed you, Fargo—you and that blamed Indian. You got more lives'n a cat. Yes, you have."

The old woman at the stove glanced at Fargo. "You look pretty cold, mister. There's fresh coffee here. You're welcome to it."

"Thanks, ma'am," Fargo replied. "I could sure use it."

The old woman brought Fargo the coffee. He took it from her and turned to the one-legged gent with the shotgun. "I see you caught up with these two," he said.

The old man's eyes narrowed. "You know 'em?"

"Yes," Fargo admitted. "I know 'em."

"Friends of yours?"

"Not likely."

"You a lawman?"

"No, but I have a warrant for their arrest."

"Well, we got 'em now," the man said with some satisfaction.

"Yes, you have. What are you planning on doing with them?"

The old man grinned. "Hell, when we caught them, Ma and I were all fired up to shoot them. But now we're not sure. Killin' in cold blood ain't our style."

"What's your name, old-timer?"

"Henry Smith—and this here's my woman, Mrs. Smith. You mind tellin' me what you're doin' up here in the middle of nowhere, with winter howlin' all around?"

"I'm looking for these two."

"Well, you found 'em, all right. But if you're lookin' for their trunk filled with gold and jewelry, I don't know where they hid it—and if I did, I sure wouldn't be tellin' you."

"It's not the gold I'm after, Smith. I told you. It's the Clemms. I'm taking them back to Fort Larned, Kansas. There's a rope waiting for them both."

"I wouldn't doubt it," said Smith. "These

Clemms are the meanest bunch of killers I ever tangled with."

"From the looks of things around here, it appears you four are all that's left from that wagon train."

"That's right," Smith admitted.

"What happened? The Clemms kill the others for their valuables?"

"That's the way Ma and me figured it."

"And then, when they ran out of food, they came after you."

"That's the pure truth of it, mister. We had the only food left. We would have shared it with them, but they was greedy. When they came for us, Ma and I made like we was asleep. I shot Ma Clemm in the stomach with my derringer. She made such a commotion I had the chance I needed to grab this here shotgun from Aaron's hand. Now it's turnabout."

"And that's fair play, ain't it mister?" said the old lady.

"Sure is," said Fargo.

"Lies," cried Pa Clemm. "Every word lies, Fargo! Let us loose now and we'll go full shares on what's in our trunk."

"That so?" asked Fargo.

"Sure," said Aaron, his eyes glittering at the thought. "These two crazy fools don't care about money. But I tell you there's thousands in that trunk. Gold coin! Silver! Rings! Bracelets! And half of it's yours, I tell you."

"Aaron's tellin' the truth, Fargo," said Pa Clemm.

"I don't doubt he is."

"Then grab that shotgun away from that old fool and free us. We'll take you to the trunk. You can't find it, less'n we take you to it."

"And you'll show me where it is?"

"Sure!"

"That a promise?"

Hope flooded Pa Clemm's eyes. "You got our solemn word."

"Pa," said Fargo, "if you took me to that trunk, I'd make you and your boy eat what's in there. Every coin, every brooch, every necklace, bracelet, every sack of gold. And if it wouldn't go down, I'd ram it down your gullets with the barrel of my Sharps. When I got finished with you two, you'd jingle when you walked. If you *could* walk, that is."

Pa and Aaron looked away from the cold fury in Fargo's eyes, aware he meant every word. They sagged sullenly back into the corner.

"Put down that shotgun, Henry," said his wife. "You know darn well you ain't goin' to shoot this feller."

At that moment Red Shirt stepped through the doorway, his Colt pointing at Smith. The old man sighed and lowered his weapon. Fargo took it gently from him and snapped it open. It was fully loaded. He snapped it shut and handed it back to the old man.

"I find Ma Clemm," Red Shirt told Fargo. "She frozen stiff in wooden box."

"What about Melody Clemm? See any sign of her?"

Red Shirt shook his head.

Fargo turned to the Smiths. "Where's Melody?"

"She escaped after we took these two," the old man said.

"You mean *you* let her go," snapped Mrs. Smith. "And all it took was one night with her."

"Now, Ma!"

"Don't you try to tell me no different."

Smith shrugged. "Okay, I won't. But you sure ain't been willin' to spend a night like that with me."

"Pshaw!" The old woman blushed. "I'm too old, and you know it."

"Well, Melody, she *warn't* too old. And when I was with her, neither was I." As Smith spoke, he winked at Fargo.

"She's gone, then," Fargo said. "That right?"

"Yep."

"You got any idea which way she was headed?"

"If I knew, I'd tell you. She's a dangerous woman." He chuckled as he recalled. "She near killed me that night—not that I'm complainin', mind."

"Looks like we'll be taking these two prisoners off your hands," Fargo told Smith, "and you and your wife better come with us, too. I don't see as how you got much future up here."

"Come with you?" Smith repeated. "In this weather?"

"You'll have to keep bundled up. That's for sure."

"I don't think Ma could make it," Smith said. "It's a long way down them steep cliffs. I don't see how you two made it up here."

"And where would we go?" asked Mrs. Smith.

"We just left a wagon train on its way to California. It'll be some distance from here by now. But we could catch up to it."

"That's where we was goin', sure enough," Smith admitted sadly. "But I don't think Mrs. Smith and I are up to goin' anywhere now."

"Stay here and you'll starve to death or freeze to death. Unpleasant deaths, both of them."

Smith glanced at his wife. "He's right," he told her. "The woodpile we got from tearing up them wagons is sure goin' fast."

"Well, if you think so, Henry."

Smith looked back at Fargo. "Guess maybe Ma and I'll be goin' with you, then."

Fargo nodded briskly. "Good. Get dressed as warm as you can and take as little as you can. The worst part of it will be climbing down off this peak. We can't use the trail your crazy wagon master used to get you up here. It's at least ten feet deep in snow by now."

As Smith and his wife vanished into a side room, Fargo went over to Pa Clemm and Aaron and slashed through the rawhide strips tied about their ankles, then untied the rawhide bind-

157

ing their wrists, retying them with their hands in front of them.

"We can't get down this mountain with our hands tied like this," Pa Clemm protested.

"You'll just have to do the best you can."

"What we goin' to wear?" Aaron bleated. "It's cold out there!"

"Where's your things?"

"In what's left of our wagon."

"Which one was that?"

"The last one in line."

Fargo glanced at Red Shirt. The Indian disappeared out the door, returning not long after with a pile of duds. Fargo untied the two prisoners' hands to allow them to climb into extra pants and shirts. They didn't have wool cloth caps, so they wound scarves about their heads instead. Despite the two men's protests, as soon as they were dressed, Fargo tied the rawhide securely around their wrists once more.

The Smiths reentered the room so heavily wrapped in clothes Fargo was afraid it would make them too clumsy for the climb down the mountainside, so he had them remove a few of the extra sweaters and pants they had put on. He was also worried about the strength of the crutch Smith had fashioned for himself.

Pointing to it, he asked him, "You think that'll hold up?"

"Had it for two years now. It's made of hickory. Suits me fine."

"Then let's go."

When they emerged from the tunnel, they found themselves stepping out into what appeared to be a new storm. Bending his head into the shrill wind, Fargo moved up the steep slope ahead of the others. Red Shirt kept to the rear behind the Clemms, Smith's loaded shotgun in his hand. As an additional safeguard, Fargo had taken the precaution of tying the Clemms to each other with a rope looped around their necks.

The snow that had fallen since they entered the shelter formed a softer, looser layer over the frozen crust beneath it. As a result their booted feet kept plunging down through the crust, slowing them considerably. Meanwhile, the wind whipped the snow into a swirling curtain of white that nearly blinded them as they pulled themselves past the wagons. Soon Fargo was spending most of his time helping Smith as the old man's hickory crutch kept disappearing into the drifts, causing him to sink deep into the snow as he probed desperately for it. Soon, their progress up the steep wall of snow in the face of a brutal, snow-laden wind became a torturous journey—well beyond what Fargo had expected when he proposed it to the Smiths.

But at last they reached the crest. Here the wind was stronger, but it carried less snow. Looking back down, Fargo saw that the trail the wagons had been following was completely blocked off, the snow now drifting over the tops of the abandoned wagons. It would not be long, Fargo realized, before everything on the trail below him would be buried as the wind-whipped snow sifted down from the rim above.

Everything, including that trunk full of loot the Clemms had been lugging across America.

Red Shirt cried out. Fargo turned. A dark shape hurled itself at him through the snow, catching him high on the shoulder and knocking him back into a drift. He felt his Sharps being twisted from his hand. Reaching up, he tried to wrest it from Aaron Clemm, but the fellow swung the stock and caught Fargo on the chin. As Fargo went slamming back into the drift, he heard Aaron fire the gun at Red Shirt.

Immediately Red Shirt's shotgun thundered, both barrels. Aaron was flung back, his father—still attached to him by the rope—going with him. The two men started plunging and rolling back down the slope toward the wagons. Fargo shook off his wooziness and pulled himself upright to catch sight of the two men. The Clemms, struggling to keep on their feet, were heading for what looked like a cave dug into the wall of snow on the slope above the last wagon. There, evidently, was where they had hidden their treasure. The two men were still linked by the rope and their hands were still bound. Aaron was not doing too well, his father having to stop constantly to pull him to his feet and drag him along.

They were almost to the cave when a high, cracking sound filled the air. It was like a gunshot. The Clemms looked up. A portion of the snow bank high above them shifted, then crumbled. With a sudden, awesome roar, a great, frothing lip of snow swept down toward the two men. They tried to run out from under it, but in seconds the avalanche swallowed them up, then swept on toward the wagons. Silence came abruptly. The wagons had vanished, a fresh sheet of snow covering them completely, its surface lumpy and pocked with the swarm of snowballs it had spawned on its plunge down the slope.

"You all right, Red Shirt?" Fargo called.

He could not see the Indian because of a sudden, swirling curtain of snow. Red Shirt loomed up a few feet from him, stepping closer through the snow, his eyes alight with pure satisfaction.

"Aaron miss me," Red Shirt announced. "But I not miss him, I think."

"You caught him, all right. The snow did the rest."

Beside Fargo, standing in a drift up to her waist, Mrs. Smith plucked at his coat. "Are they dead?" she whispered in awe. "Both of them?"

"Buried alive in that snowbank," Fargo told her. "Not a nice death. But then they weren't very nice people."

Beside her, Smith nodded, panting for breath. "It was that fool treasure chest of theirs. Put quite a store by it. Couldn't bear to leave it behind."

"Well, they didn't," Fargo remarked grimly. "It's buried with them."

*   *   *

It happened without warning.

One second Smith was at Fargo's side, muttering under his breath as he fought his way through the drifts, the next he was tumbling headlong after his crutch. It had struck a patch of ice and gone flying out from under him. Fargo leapt after him, just managing to catch the tail of his heavy jacket. They slipped farther down until they came to a halt on the brow of an ice-covered ridge. Fargo glimpsed a jagged wasteland of snow and ice hundreds of feet below them.

Turning his head carefully, he saw Red Shirt attempting to pick his way down the slope toward them. But Fargo's and Smith's bodies had swept the slope clear of snow, opening up a glaring, extremely slippery stretch of ice.

"Stay back, Red Shirt," Fargo told him. "It's too slippery."

Red Shirt pulled back. Reaching out then, the Indian pulled Mrs. Smith back also. She was peering down at her husband, obviously terrified.

Fargo looked down at Smith. "Can you work your way back up to me?"

"I got nothin' to use! My crutch is gone!"

"Forget the crutch. Use your hands. Push yourself back up here to me."

Smith tried. But his gloved hands slipped fruitlessly on the ice, and the effort caused his entire body to pull heavily on Fargo. Both men inched closer to the abyss yawning beneath them. Luckily, with his free hand Fargo found—just under the snow—a crack in the rock. Clasping its edge, he kept himself from slipping any farther.

"Hold still," Fargo told Smith. "Don't move. I'll pull you up!"

But as Fargo tried to do so, his near-frozen hand could not hold Smith's jacket tightly enough and it began to slip slowly, inexorably out of his grasp. Fargo was about to let go of the crack with his other hand and grab Smith's collar when Smith's jacket pulled free of his grasp. With a startled cry, Smith slipped over the edge. Once, twice he turned completely in midair, then vanished into a dark crevasse, the snow he dislodged flowing in after him. In less than a minute the icy cavern into which he had vanished was filled with snow.

Fargo heard a scream above him. Glancing back up the slope, he saw Mrs. Smith struggling with Red Shirt. Twice she broke free of the Indian's grasp and tried to fling herself after her husband, but each time Red Shirt was able to pull her back. At last, exhausted from struggling with the powerful Indian, she sagged, sobbing, to the ground.

Only then did Fargo think it safe to climb back up.

By the time they found a shelter for the night—still high in the white, screaming wilderness of rock and snow—Mrs. Smith had become a dull, half-frozen ball of snow and ice. Her hands were nearly frozen, her cheeks glazed from frozen tears. They kept her between them as they bedded down in the tent, the wind howling about their flimsy shelter like some demented beast. Before letting her fall off to sleep, they rubbed the old woman's hands between theirs, managing finally to coax the circulation back into them. They gently picked the ice off her face.

Through all this the old woman said nothing, staring eerily past them or through them. Whatever her eyes saw, Fargo realized, it was not him or Red Shirt. Her inner eye was seeing other, sunnier days. Or perhaps she was back as a young girl with her own family. One thing was for sure, however: wherever she was, it was far from this frigid rampart of ice and snow.

Wondering whatever in the world had induced this old, feeble couple to pull up stakes and head for California, Fargo curled into his sugan like a sled dog and fell asleep. Awakening suddenly around midnight, he opened his eyes and saw Mrs. Smith sitting bolt upright. She appeared alert, her eyes crafty as she leaned forward out of her blankets. Putting her shoulders down, she pushed herself out of the tent. Fargo was about to grab her and pull her back when he saw Red Shirt's dark eyes watching him. The Indian shook his head.

Fargo peered out through the tent flap at Mrs. Smith. She had pushed herself upright and was struggling through the drifts like a small, shambling bear. The moon's light was sporadic as the wind-driven clouds scudded across its face, but for a while Fargo could see clearly the old woman's tiny, laboring figure as she struggled on up the slope through the snow-driven wind on her journey back to the spot where her husband had gone over. She would never make it that far, Fargo realized. But that did not matter.

After one particularly dense curtain of snow was flung up between her and Fargo, he looked for her in vain. Somewhere in that howling night she had rejoined her husband.

10

A day later they reached the spot where they had left their horses and led them on down the mountainside until they reached the timberline. The snow here was constant, but light. Before mounting up, Fargo peered once more up at the peak. It was lost in swirling clouds. He heard faint rumblings of thunder and caught the gleam of lightning deep in the cloud's underbelly. From now until spring those mountain flanks would remain a forbidding land of ice and snow, and one peak in particular a grim, howling tombstone for the Smiths and the Clemms.

Now, only Melody Clemm was left.

Red Shirt cut ahead of him into the timber, Fargo following. By the time they made their night camp, the snow was behind them, and what snow remained on the ground was wet and heavy from the day's sun. Dark patches of ground were everywhere. If they kept on, Fargo realized, they might possibly overtake the wagon train in a week or so.

After they had eaten their supper of jerky and beans topped off with steaming black coffee, Fargo fed the fire with fresh kindling and sat back on the log he had dragged over. Holding his cup of coffee in both hands to warm them, he glanced across the fire at Red Shirt.

"How are you feeling, Red Shirt?"

It was not a good question to ask an Indian. Red Shirt returned his gaze with no hint of what he was thinking, and shrugged.

"You satisfied, now Pa Clemm and Aaron are gone?"

"No," the Indian replied shortly, sipping his steaming coffee.

"How come?"

"Melody Clemm. We not find her yet."

"You think we should go back after her through the South Pass?"

"She go that way?"

"I figure she might."

"Why?"

"To get help at Red Gap for her pa and brother."

Still sipping his coffee, Red Shirt said, "Maybe you right. We go back."

"You won't need to," said a voice from the darkness behind Red Shirt.

Glancing over, Fargo saw Melody Clemm step into the ring of firelight, a six-gun gleaming in her hand.

With the suddenness of a striking rattler, Red Shirt spun about and flung the contents of his cup into Melody Clemm's face. As the searing liquid struck her, Melody screamed and staggered back. Red Shirt rushed her. But Melody managed to lift her gun and send a round into the charging Indian. His momentum carried him into her, however, and she was flung to the ground as Red Shirt collapsed beside her, his body writhing in pain.

As Melody struggled to get to her feet, Fargo snatched the revolver out of her hand. She came at him with hooked fingers. Fargo slapped her so hard she went flying into a wet snowbank and lay there, dazed, her hand held up to her stinging face. Fargo bent to examine Red Shirt's wound. He didn't like what he saw. The bullet had smashed into Red Shirt's chest. It would need to be removed—and soon.

But the only doctor Fargo knew of who could perform such an operation was in that wagon train descending through the mountains, perhaps a full week ahead of him by now. Fargo walked over to Melody and searched her for any further weapons. He found a knife big enough to cut out a buffalo's heart and some cartridges for the Colt she had just used. He pocketed the cartridges and stuck the Colt and knife in his belt, then hauled her to her feet.

"My eyes," she told him. "That crazy Indian burned my eyes. I'm blind."

Fargo doubled up his fist and started to swing

on her, aiming for her chin. She ducked deftly to one side, cursing him as she did so.

"Seems to me you can see all right," Fargo remarked coldly.

"Damn you!"

"Where's your horse?"

"I ain't got one. Why do you think it's taken me so long to get this far?"

"I never thought about it. Help me lift Red Shirt into his saddle. Then you get on behind and hold him up."

"Why the hell should I?"

"Because if you don't, I'll cut your heart out with your own knife and feed it to the vultures."

"You wouldn't," she said, her eyes narrowing warily.

"Try me."

"All right," she muttered. "But where we goin'?"

"To catch up to that wagon train we left. There's a doctor there, a feller you know pretty well. Wilder."

"He's there? You mean he made it?"

"Just barely."

"He has me to thank for it, then. I was the one helped him escape."

"So he said."

"It's true!"

"I'm not arguing it. Now give me a hand."

Grudgingly, Melody helped Fargo lift Red Shirt up onto his horse. Then, hiking up her filthy, torn skirt, she climbed up behind the

Indian. Fargo gave her the reins. Holding them with one hand, she tucked her other hand around the Indian's waist.

"Phew," she said, looking down at Fargo. "He stinks."

"Like a good Indian should. Go on down this trail. I'll be right behind you."

Despite Melody's protests, they rode continuously, night and day, stopping only to rest the horses and snatch a few winks of sleep. When at last they glimpsed the wagon train ahead of them, Red Shirt was in pretty bad shape, and both Fargo and Melody were exhausted.

Overtaking the last wagon, Fargo left Red Shirt in it. With Melody riding beside him, they kept going until they pulled abreast of Helen's wagon. Up on the seat beside her, the reins in his hand, sat Doc Wilder, looking much better than he had the last time Fargo had seen him.

At sight of Melody Clemm, both Helen and Wilder froze.

Without bothering to explain Melody's presence, Fargo called, "Wilder, get back to the last wagon. Red Shirt's in there. He's got a bullet in him."

Without a word, Wilder nodded, gave the reins to Helen, and jumped down.

Fargo spurred ahead with Melody until he reached the lead wagon. "Pull up," he called. "Doc Wilder's got a patient he needs to work on."

Without a word of argument, Hunter turned

his wagon onto a stretch of meadow just off the trail.

Around dusk, a weary Doc Wilder sat down beside Fargo and accepted the cup of coffee Helen handed him. In the fire's flickering light, Fargo searched Wilder's face for some clue as to Red Shirt's condition. He saw only fatigue.

"I got the bullet out," Wilder told him. "It wasn't easy. I must've poked around in that poor man's chest for fifteen minutes, and the poor son of a bitch didn't utter a sound. Then I poured fresh whiskey into the wound to fight any infection. That should've made him howl like a coyote. It didn't."

"Indian's don't say much, Wilder," Fargo told him. "Will he be all right?"

"Oh, he'll live. It'd be easier to kill a grizzly."

Fargo leaned back and took a deep breath, feeling better at once. Putting down his coffee, he took out a cigar and lit it.

"He wants to see you," said Wilder.

"You mean he's awake?"

Wilder nodded.

Fargo got up and walked over to Helen's wagon, where Red Shirt had been taken after the wagons halted. Climbing in, he found Red Shirt awake, his anthracite eyes gleaming in the darkness.

"The doc says you're gonna live," Fargo told him.

Red Shirt only nodded.

"Why don't you get some sleep now."

"First I ask you. What you do with that woman?"

"Melody Clemm?"

"It was her people kill my people. And now she almost kill me."

"Don't worry. I'm bringing her back to Fort Larned for trial."

"That will be long ride with such a woman."

"I'm not looking forward to it."

"Let me kill her."

"Can't do that, Red Shirt."

"White man's law?"

Fargo nodded.

"I must avenge my people."

"Hell, look at it this way, Red Shirt. Four members of her family are dead already. She's the only one left."

"And Red Shirt want her."

"So you want me to keep her here until you're ready to kill her."

Red Shirt grunted eagerly. "I will be ready soon. In one day, maybe two."

Fargo shook his head. "I can't, Red Shirt."

Red Shirt looked at him closely for a long moment, as if he were trying to figure out why Fargo would not go along with him. Then he let his head drop back onto the pillow and closed his eyes.

Fargo watched him for a moment longer. When he was sure Red Shirt was asleep, he climbed down out of the wagon and went in search of Melody Clemm.

She was where he had left her, apparently asleep under a tree, her wrists tied securely behind her, both ankles bound tightly. He bent to test the rawhide binding her wrists and noted the blood between the rawhide and her skin. Judging from the freshness of the blood, she must have been struggling frantically only moments before he appeared.

He went down on one knee beside her . . . and waited. After a moment more of bluffing sleep, Melody opened her eyes and stared at him, her eyes alive with a fierce hatred.

"The rawhide too tight, is it?"

"Yes."

"Good."

"Will you loosen it?"

"No."

"What do you plan to do to me?"

"Well, if I can keep Red Shirt from killing you, I'll take you to Fort Larned and hand you over to the authorities for a proper hanging."

"They'd never hang a woman!"

"This one they will."

She spat upon him.

He ducked away, dabbing at his face with his handkerchief. Then he left her.

A scream awakened Fargo. He had been asleep under a cottonwood. Scrambling out of his sugan, he snatched up his Colt and ran toward the sound. It was Helen screaming, and the sound of her cries sent shivers up his spine.

Under the tree where Melody Clemm had been bound, Helen was bent over Doc Wilder's sprawled figure, Wilder's big Colt in her hand. She was sobbing, her boy beside her. The youngster looked white-faced and very frightened as he stared down at Doc Wilder. Apparently Wilder and the boy had become pretty close these past weeks.

Fargo bent over the doc. Wilder was just coming around.

"She stabbed me," he managed, "with my own scalpel."

"You going to be all right?"

"She caught me in the side. Twice. If I can stop the bleeding, I'll make it."

"What happened?"

"She complained about the rawhide biting into her wrists, said they were too tight. So I cut them off her."

"You freed her?"

"I didn't mean to. I was going to bandage her wrists, then tie her up again."

"Only she never gave you the chance."

"She was as fast as a scorpion," he admitted, wincing suddenly from the pain. He looked at Helen. "Get some bandages, Helen. I'm getting pretty weak. I mustn't lose any more blood."

Helen hurried back to her wagon as a growing crowd of settlers gathered in a circle around them. Fargo stood up and peered into the darkness surrounding the wagons. Melody Clemm was gone now. And Fargo had no doubt it was

174

Wilder's fool fascination for her black, evil heart that had brought him out here to her in the first place.

"Fargo!"

It was Helen. He ran to her wagon. She was waiting for him, her face drawn and white. "It's Red Shirt."

"What do you mean?"

"He's dead."

"Melody?"

"Who else?" she hissed.

Fargo vaulted up into the wagon to examine Red Shirt. A clean, red line had been traced across his throat. The scalpel had been wielded with such precision that Fargo doubted if Red Shirt had even awakened as the blade sliced through his jugular.

A screaming shadow materialized out of the corner of the wagon. Fargo turned as Melody Clemm lunged, her right hand striking out at him with incredible speed. Fargo felt something slicing into his side. He twisted away. Flinging her right arm around his neck, Melody jabbed once again with the scalpel. A sharp, paralyzing pain lanced deep into Fargo's side. He found it difficult to breathe and, gasping, fell to the floor of the wagon.

Turning his head, he saw Melody looming over him, the scalpel upraised, readying herself to bring it down for the final *coup de grace*. A shot rang out. Melody's body shook, then straightened. Another shot thundered, and then another.

175

The third round brought Melody down finally. She slumped heavily to the wagon floor, her beautiful, seductive eyes staring sightlessly at him.

As he drifted off into a painful sleep, he saw Helen lowering Wilder's Colt and reminded himself with some relief that he wouldn't have to take Melody Clemm back with him all the way to Fort Larned.

Hell! He might not even get there himself.

Jan Sheridan was bent over her ledger at the front desk when Fargo entered the hotel. She was so busy and he was so quiet, she did not look up until he paused before the front desk and inquired about a room for the night.

"Skye," Jan cried, stepping quickly out from behind the desk and flinging her arms about his neck.

As she hugged him, he winced through his smile.

She stepped back quickly. "You're hurt?"

"Nothing serious. I'm on the mend."

"Where's your friend—and the Indian?"

"It's a long story. Can we visit awhile?"

"Why, of course!"

She turned back to the desk and palmed the bell twice. A young bellhop materialized on the second-floor landing and hurried down the stairs. Jan told him to hold down the desk and that she wasn't to be disturbed. A moment later, she was helping Fargo out of his buckskins, listening to his story.

At the end of it, she stopped his tale with a kiss. Gratefully, he kissed her in return. Much, much later, they had their supper brought in to them.

Still in bed beside Jan, the meal finished, Fargo asked about Sheriff Beaman.

Jan laughed, delighted. "You don't have to worry about him," she said, scooting up so that her back was resting against a pillow. She was eating an apple. "He was so anxious to find you, he rode his horse into the ground. It foundered and sent him flying."

"Hurt bad, was he?"

"No one thought so at first. But the fall left him daft. I'm sure of it."

"How do you know?"

"For one thing, he talks to himself. For another, he winces every time he passes a horse."

Fargo laughed.

"So now he hides in his office, and if he has to go anywhere, he walks. We'll have ourselves a new sheriff after the next election. Skye Fargo, I nominate you to run for sheriff. What do you say?"

"I'm heading back to Kansas, Fort Larned."

"I can't talk you into staying put for a while?"

"Afraid not."

"Well, then," she said, finishing her apple and scooting down to rest her cheek on his massive chest, "thanks for stopping by on your way."

"I had to thank you, Jan. You saved our necks."

"I was glad to do it. But I'm sorry to hear about Barrows—and that Indian. I liked him."

"So did I."

She kissed him then, impulsively. Instantly it became something else, something far more urgent—for both of them.

Fargo lit his third cigar as Lieutenant Becker refilled his glass with bourbon. Thanking him, Fargo leaned back in his chair and took up the glass.

"That's all of it," he told Fort Larned's commanding officer. "Not a pretty tale, I admit."

"At least," said the lieutenant, "we won't have to worry about the Clemms anymore—thanks to you."

"And thanks to Helen Shellabarger," Fargo reminded Becker. "It was her that put an end to Melody Clemm's career."

Becker was sucking on his pipe, his dark eyes gleaming with appreciation of Fargo's remarkable tale. "It's too bad about Barrows and that Indian. A stiff price to pay to rid the world of the Clemms." He paused for a while, puffing on his pipe, going over in his mind what Fargo had just told him. Then he glanced at Fargo. "From what you say, it was Wilder's fault that Melody Clemm escaped that night."

"It was."

"Why did he do it, I wonder?"

"He called her a scorpion, Lieutenant," Fargo replied, "and that's what she was. She could draw any man to her, but only to bury her stinger in his heart."

"But not you."

Fargo shrugged. "I've dealt with her like before. Doc Wilder read too many books and never had to deal with a woman as fascinating or as deadly as Melody Clemm."

"He was lucky to escape with his life."

"If he hadn't, I wouldn't be here myself."

"That old couple, the Smiths. What a terrible way for them to go!"

"Maybe. You can bet I've thought a lot about them since. Still, they weren't really going anywhere. They were pretty old and frail. The way I look at it, the two of them had just about run out of time when I ran into them up there—and when Smith went, what was there left for his woman to do?"

Becker puffed on his pipe for a while, thinking. "I suppose you're right," he said at last. "I've heard of cases like that. When one goes, not long after the other one does, too. After all that time together, they aren't really two people anymore."

Fargo nodded.

Becker turned to Fargo. "And now what about you and those men you were trailing when you first came here?"

"I never got the chance to ask Melody if her family killed them or if they're still alive. But judging from her and the rest of her kin, I don't have much doubt them two were killed and robbed too."

"But you'll never know for sure."

"No, I guess I won't."

"Which means you will just have to continue your search."

"Yes."

"I don't envy you, Skye. But I wish you luck."

Fargo finished his bourbon and got to his feet. "Thanks, Lieutenant," he said, "and good luck in this here war you're off to."

"I think I'll need it," Becker responded ruefully. "It looks to me like this trouble between the states is going to take a whole lot longer to straighten out than most people figured."

Not long after, as Fargo rode out of the fort, he looked back and saw the lieutenant waving good-bye. As he rode, he found himself recalling Red Shirt's coal-black eyes and the tough nut-brown little Texan. He missed them both and felt a deep sense of loss. He would never find their like again.

His hope was that he would never find another Melody Clemm either.

LOOKING FORWARD!

**The following is the opening section
from the next novel in the exciting
Trailsman series from Signet:**

The Trailsman #55
THIEF RIVER SHOWDOWN

*Northwest Minnesota, 1860,
land of the north lakes and the north winds,
just below the Thief River . . .*

He didn't expect to see a girl there. She spelled
trouble, and she had no business being in that
saloon. But she was there.

There were saloons and there were saloons,
and then there were upholstered sewers. The
Bent Wheel Saloon was an upholstered sewer—
filthy, dark, with one long bar and a dozen battered tables, torn drapes and peeling paint. It
was a place filled with pack rats, bums and booz-
ers, men on the run, some from the world, some
from themselves. The girl was as out of place as a
spring gentian in a swamp. She was pretty in a
pert, pugnacious way, a round-cheeked face, a

little snub nose with a row of freckles on it, short brown hair. She wore a shirt of dark-green checks over Levi's, a Walker sticking from the waistband of her outfit. Not tall, she had a firm, young shape, a round little rear, and very high, almost conelike breasts.

But she was in trouble now, and he watched the trio of men that had half-surrounded her. The ringleader—a tall, thin figure, pasty-faced with a wispy excuse of a beard—grinned obscenely as he moved toward her. "You come in here, girlie, you got to give us a little feel," he said, and his hand stretched out to touch her breasts.

She knocked his hand away and held her ground. "Don't you touch me, you piece of slime," she snapped.

"Now, that's no way for you to talk, girlie. You're gonna get old Nick mad at you," the man said.

"I'll put a bullet in old Nick's gut," the girl said.

Fargo shook his head with grudging admiration. She was a tough little character. Tough but foolish. From where he sat in a corner of the saloon he saw one of the other two men circle around to come up behind her. She was completely unaware of him, all her attention on the pasty-faced man in front of her. As Fargo watched, the figure behind her sprang and pinned her arms to her side. A stocky man with a flat, broad face, he laughed harshly as he held the girl. The one who'd called himself Nick snapped his hand out, yanked the gun from the girl's waist, and sent it skittering across the floor.

"You won't be needing that, girlie." He laughed as he pressed both hands to her breasts, rubbing them back and forth as the stocky man held her. Fargo saw the girl's foot come up and lash out in a short, high kick.

"Ow," the one called Nick screamed, and clapped both hands to his groin as he sank to his knees. Fargo saw the third man rush up, a bony nose in a bony face, and smash his hand across the girl's cheek.

"Bitch," he rasped, and avoided another kick. Nick rose, pain still in his face, but his lips were drawn back in a grimace of rage.

"Take her in the back. We're going to teach her how to be nice," he ordered.

Fargo's eyes scanned the others in the saloon. Most stared into their drinks with determined indifference while a few sneaked quick glances at the three men and the girl. But no one moved to do anything more. They wouldn't, Fargo knew. They were all cut from the same cloth, all losers. Fear was a part of their inaction, as perhaps was some envy and some vicarious enjoyment. It all added up to doing nothing.

"Bastards. Let me go, damn you," Fargo heard the girl shout. She twisted, wriggled, tried to bite, but the three men held her tight as they dragged her across the floor. Two held her arms while the tall, pasty-faced one had seized a handful of her short brown hair and kept her head up. They dragged her toward a closed door at the far end of the saloon.

Fargo let a deep sigh escape him as he rose to his feet. "Why the hell was she in the saloon in the first place?" he muttered quietly as he eyed the guns the trio wore on their hips. The pasty-faced one wore an Army percussion Colt, a slow trigger pull, he grunted inwardly. The other two had Colt Hartford Dragoon pistols, six-shot weapons but heavy in the hand and slow to draw.

"Let the girl go," he said, his voice hardly raised yet carrying with icy clarity.

The three men halted, and the pasty-faced one let go of his grip on the girl's hair as he moved to one side. Frowning, he stared at the big man with the lake-blue eyes and the thick, black hair.

"What'd you say?" he growled.

"I said, let the girl go," Fargo repeated.

"Who the hell are you?" the man barked.

"Name's Fargo ... Skye Fargo," the Trailsman said almost affably.

"You know her?" the pasty-faced one queried.

"Not yet. But I'm getting tired waiting. Let her go, scum," Fargo said, his voice growing crisp.

He saw disbelief slide across the man's pasty

face and then spiraling anger. "You're crazy," the man uttered.

"Maybe," Fargo said.

"I'm goin' to shoot your damn head off, mister," the man said.

"You couldn't shoot the ass off an elephant in front of you," Fargo said as his eyes bored into the man's face. But with his peripheral vision, he saw the man's hand move, his fingers spread out as he brought his arm in line with the holster at his hip. His eyes flicked to the other two men still holding the girl, an instant, silent message. His fingers stiffened and Fargo smiled to himself. Like most stupid gunslingers, the man had given himself away. His hand flashed upward as he went for his gun. It was still curled around the butt of the pistol when Fargo's shot blew his chest apart in a shower of red.

The man fell back into one of the tables, bringing it to the floor with him. But Fargo had already swung the Colt around to the other two. One of them had used the precious split seconds to get his gun out of its holster. He had only raised it halfway into firing position when Fargo's second shot exploded. The stocky figure half-spun around as he swore in pain, clutching at his shoulder as the gun fell from his fingers. He staggered sideways with one hand on his shoulder, fell to his knees, and slumped against one of the tables.

Fargo's gun was on the third man, who had flung himself to the floor with the girl and lay half under her, his gun held against her temple. "Back off or she gets it," he snarled.

Fargo hesitated, his mind racing. Even if he got a bullet into the man, the scum's finger on the trigger would automatically jerk, and the girl was dead. He grimaced and backed a half-dozen steps. The man kept the girl half atop him, the gun against her temple, as he began to push himself backward across the saloon floor toward the door. Fargo, eyes narrowed, the Colt ready to fire, gauged distance, angle, movement, and decided again that it was too risky. The man's finger had only to tighten on the trigger, the muzzle of the gun flat against the girl's temple.

Fargo remained motionless as the man reached the door of the saloon, pushed himself to his feet, and brought the girl up with him. His gun continued to stay against her temple as he backed out of the saloon. Fargo held back until he heard the sound of hoofbeats galloping away. He streaked across the dingy little saloon and out onto the street to see the man racing out of town on a brown quarterhorse with the girl on her stomach across the saddle in front of him.

Fargo vaulted onto the magnificent Ovaro as he yanked the reins free of the hitching post with one hand. It only took moments to race to the end of the few buildings that made up the town. He saw the horse streaking on ahead of him through a line of alders. He started after the fleeing horseman, reached the beginning of the alders, and let the man see him rein to a halt. He waited a moment and slowly turned the Ovaro around, aware that the man watched with quick glances. Fargo headed the horse back toward town at a walk, halted again only when the fleeing horseman finally disappeared from sight.

Then he whirled the Ovaro around again and set off across the low hill that rose west of the line of alders. He raced the horse through huge northern red oak, keeping the alders in sight on his left. The hill rose, flattened out, and stayed heavy with the red oak as he turned the horse west toward the alders, which now continued in a line slightly below where he rode. He drew closer to the trees and spotted the fleeing horseman as he moved through open patches. The man had slowed to a trot, but still had the girl lying on her stomach across the saddle.

Fargo swung north, paralleled the horse just below, keeping out of sight in the cover of the red oaks. The man kept riding, plainly taking no chances on being caught. He watched as the alders began to thin, finally ended in a stand of silver balsam that edged a small lake. The purple-gray haze of dusk began to slide across the countryside when Fargo saw the man halt, slide from the horse, and pull the girl from the saddle. He flung her to the ground roughly, and she rolled once. She came up on her elbows to glare back.

Fargo moved the Ovaro down the gentle tree-covered slope as he drew the big Sharps rifle from its saddle holster. He brought the horse to a halt at the end of the red oaks where a short hill of low brush slanted down to where the man faced the girl.

"That big bastard thought you were worth shootin' for but not chasin' after," Fargo heard the man say with a snarling laugh.

"Maybe he's still coming," the girl said.

"He quit," the man said. "I kept lookin' back. He didn't show again. Now I'm going to finish what Nick started, you little bitch."

Fargo watched as he moved toward the girl, whose hand came up with a fistful of soil she slammed into the man's face. "Goddamn," the man spit out, blinked, wiped an arm across his face.

The girl was on her feet, running up the hillside, her legs churning as the man started after her. Fargo watched as she glanced back at her pursuer for an instant, broke her momentum, tried to dig in harder, and slipped on a loose stone. She went down on one knee and recovered quickly, but the man was able to get his hand around her left ankle. He slipped as she pulled, but he held his grip and the girl went down again. "Goddamn little bitch," he cursed as he yanked, and she slid down to him.

But she turned as he pulled her, flipped half onto her back, and drove one foot forward down, down. The man turned his face away just in time to avoid the full force of the kick, but he caught part of the blow on the top of his head. It broke his hold on the girl's ankle, and Fargo watched her roll past her attacker, half-fall down the slope, and regain her feet. She was racing for the man's horse, he saw with a smile of admiration. She was one little hellion, full of fight, fire, and guts. He saw the man get to his feet and heard his bellow of rage.

"No, you don't, you goddamn little bitch. I'll kill you first," the man roared as the girl neared his horse.

Fargo saw her throw a glance back, her eyes wide with fear as she saw the man yank at his gun. But she kept running, the horse hardly a half-dozen yards away. Fargo saw the man raise his gun and take aim at the girl's running figure, and he raised the big Sharps to his shoulder. The rifle shot resounded down the slope as though it were a small, sharp clap of thunder, and the man seemed to go into a strange little dance as he whirled in a half-circle, tottered, and pitched forward to roll down the slope. He stopped rolling almost at the edge of the small lake, and Fargo saw the girl, frozen in place, look back with her eyes wide. She stared at the figure lying life-lessly, then slowly turned her eyes to peer up the hillside as Fargo moved the Ovaro forward into sight and came slowly down to halt in front of her.

She blinked, swallowed, and her pert, snub-nosed face finally relaxed. "I was waiting to feel the bullet when I heard the shot," she said.

Fargo swung from the horse and slid the rifle back into its saddle holster.

"Thanks," she added. "Such a dumb little word for so much. I owe you."

He took her in with a long, careful appraisal for the first time and decided his first impression held. She was damned pretty in her own pugna-cious way, her breasts so full and high they pushed proudly into the dark-green shirt, her fig-ure compact and firm. She radiated a kind of energetic vitality even standing still.

"You put up a damn good fight, honey. You're a real hellcat," he finally said. "But going into that saloon was pretty damn dumb. Even the town whores would think twice about going in there."

She met his remarks with her own appraisal as she let round brown eyes take in the chiseled handsomeness of the big man's face, the power in his shoulders and arms.

"What the hell were you doing in there?"

Fargo continued, not without a surge of irritation.

"I went to meet you," she said.

Fargo frowned as he stared at the girl's calm, snub-nosed face. "You what?" he muttered.

"I was there to meet you," she said again.

His frown deepened, pulling his thick black eyebrows lower. "How the hell did you know I'd be there?" he questioned.

"You were supposed to meet somebody there, weren't you?" she answered.

"Yes, but it sure as hell wasn't you," he snapped.

"I know that," she said with a touch of disdain.

"Who are you? What the hell's this all about?" Fargo asked.

"I'm Trudy Keyser," she said.

"Is that supposed to mean something to me, because it sure as hell doesn't," Fargo growled.

"No. Not yet, anyway," she said.

"Then start explaining, Trudy Keyser. Why'd you come to that rat's nest to meet me?" Fargo questioned.

"I want to hire you. I've real good money for it," the girl said.

"Then you've just wasted your time coming here, and my time saving your little ass. I've got a job," he snapped.

"I know that, too," she said, the touch of disdain in her voice again. "You're on your way to Thief River Junction. This won't interfere with that."

Fargo felt the stab of surprise again. There was surely nothing secret about his destination, but he hadn't expected this feisty, determined girl to know that. "Why won't it interfere?" he questioned cautiously.

"You can teach me on the way," she said.

"Teach you what?" He frowned.

"Teach me everything you know. Teach me to be a Trailsman," Trudy Keyser said.

Fargo stared at her round brown eyes, which remained absolutely steady. He shook his head slowly as amazement curled up inside him. "Honey, you are plumb crazy," he said.